The Antarean Odyssey

This is the story about the birth of a people and the fiery end of their home-world. It is a story about adventure, love, heartbreak, sorrow and of overcoming difficult and dangerous situations.

The Antarean Odyssey

The Labors of Jonathan

Book One

One evening Jonathan Wright overhears a conversation about a world wide cartel, an interstellar trade agreement, and aliens called Altruscans.

The Antarean Odyssey

The Original Four

Book Two

Book two is about four girls coming from diverse cultures and backgrounds, and they are the beginning of the Antarean people

The Antarean Odyssey

Loss of Eden

Book Three

The ending of childhood might feel like to loss of Eden: It is time for the four to meet the world.

The story is about an expedition that goes terribly wrong. Sabrina races home against time and death only to find a deserted ship. The Antares is only manned by androids.

The Antarean Odyssey

Starship Trefayne

Book Four

Sabrina didn't mind leaving Acheron. But she was not too crazy about having to drop her studies and then, being a guinea pig integrating a Chiron ship. The Chirons claimed that their PSI awareness made it a hardship to interact with anyone not having the ability to shield their emotions. Well, Sabrina thought, I'll find out if that's just a bunch of crap or not.

If Sargon thought to have Sabrina safely on the Trefayne, he will soon learn otherwise.

Books to be published are
The Antarean Odyssey
Misalliances
Book Five

The Antarean Odyssey
Assignment Earth
Book Six

The Antarean Odyssey

Trefayne

Inge Blanton

iUniverse, Inc.
New York   Bloomington

The Antarean Odyssey
Trefayne

iUniverse books may be ordered through booksellers or by contacting:

iUniverse
1663 Liberty Drive
Bloomington, IN 47403
www.iuniverse.com
1-800-Authors (1-800-288-4677)

ISBN: 978-1-4401-8399-7 (pbk)
ISBN: 978-1-4401-8400-0 (ebook)

Printed in the United States of America

iUniverse rev. date: 11/9/2009

When her husband retired for the Army, Inge Blanton settled with her family in Oklahoma. After her seven children finished college, Blanton attended the University of Oklahoma and graduated in 1994

The Antarean Odyssey

Book Four

Starship Trefayne

Chapter 1

There was a distinct jar as the shuttle docked with the Starship Trefayne.

Sabrina looked at her timepiece. Good, she thought, right on time. I would have hated to be late boarding a Chiron ship. First impressions might matter.

Snatching up her duffle bag, she marched off the shuttle behind two Chirons. It was her first time on a starship, and as an afterthought she added, as an ensign. She didn't mind leaving Acheron behind with its intrigues and troubles, but was not pleased to be so abruptly ordered to drop her studies. She had planned to double her hours, and one additional year would have earned her an interstellar law degree.

Nor did she feel especially crazy about being a guinea pig for the Alliance, integrating a Chiron ship. The Chirons claimed that their PSI awareness made it a hardship to interact with anyone who did not have the ability to shield their emotions. Well, I'll find out if that's just a bunch a crap or not she thought, as she looked around the hangar-deck. Her first impression was that everything was too clean, too orderly, and too antiseptic. The walls were a dull, uniform, light-gray. Sabrina pursed her mouth. It's just as I imagined a Chiron ship to look, absolutely no personality, not like the Antares. She almost chuckled, remembering that one of the Antares' hangar-decks sported a pterodactyl. Years ago, Yoshi and Benjie had to work off accumulated demerits. Their punishment was to clean the hangar-deck. Sargon told them it better be spotless. After the boys thought their task was accomplished, they painted a pterodactyl on one of the walls with Sargon as prey in its talons. The picture of Sargon was only sketched in, but recognizable. When Yoshi and Benjie took too long returning, Sargon became concerned and went to investigate. He walked in as the two were still admiring their handiwork. Sargon never inspected the hangar deck. All he said the boys later related was good profile; good job, and walked off, leaving us speechless. Benjie had been fifteen and Yoshi, seventeen.

Reminiscing made her homesick and inattentive; Sabrina almost lost the two Chirons. They too, were ensigns, and newly assigned to the Trefayne. When the Chirons lined up in front of an officer, Sabrina followed suit. Then it was her turn to salute.

"Ensign Hennesee reporting. Permission to come aboard, Sir," she said in Galactic.

"Permission granted, Ensign Hennesee. Welcome on board the Trefayne. I am First Officer Dan." He looked at a small hand-held computer. "Your quarters are on deck five, cabin number fifty-four. As soon as you are settled, report to Chief Engineer Ethan," and he handed her a layout of the ship.

"Aye, Sir."

Sabrina saluted again, took one step back and turned. After picking up her duffel bag, she marched off, first to find the lift, and then her quarters.

Inwardly she cringed, ensign. What a comedown. On the Worldship Antares she held the hard-earned rank of commander; she was second in command.

A week ago, she received her induction into the Space Fleet of the Planetary Alliance, and became an ensign. Her chosen profession was engineering. At first, her feelings had been mixed. Getting through school in record time was something she was proud of; however, the reduction in rank was still hard to swallow. And now, she had to start at the bottom again.

But for the time being she decided to take life as it came and play along. She entered the lift and said, "Deck five." When the doors opened, there was something written in large letters on the opposite wall, and again, in smaller letters underneath, in Galactic, informing her that this was indeed deck five.

"I guess that's what the Chirons think of themselves, and then the rest of us," she mumbled in English.

"Aye lass, that's the gist of it."

Startled, Sabrina dropped her duffel bag and spun around. "What! You're not a mirage, are you?"

The Scottish burr belonged to a redheaded, broad-shouldered man with icy-blue eyes who appeared to be in his forties. He was standing to the right of the open door.

"No lass," he said, his blue eyes twinkling, "I'm real enough." He chuckled at her baffled look. "I thought to find yer, and help if need be. We Earth-people need to stick together, especially on a ship full of Chirons. I'm Ian McPherson."

"Hello, Ian McPherson," Sabrina intoned. "I thought I was the only non-Chiron on board."

"Well, I've known Estel before he became Captain of the Trefayne, and when he asked me to ship 'oot' wit' him, I agreed. We went to school together, and he kinda took a liken to me. I'm the engineer, right under the Chief Engineer. So, like I said, if ye need help, talk to me. What's yer cabin number?"

"Fifty-four."

"Turn left; it should be halfway down the corridor. Be prompt to report to Commander Ethan."

Sabrina thanked him and took the left turn, glancing back once in a while with a puzzled look. Scottish, she thought. What a crazy universe. She opened the door to her cabin and dropped her bag, staying only long enough to notice that the cabin was small, but adequate. Then she went in search of Commander Ethan.

The Commander turned out to be tall and gaunt. And, like most Chirons, with a dour expression, never a smile.

Commander Ethan took Sabrina's measure as she walked into the engine room. He had very little patience for young upstarts, especially female, and was not pleased to have one assigned to his department.

Sabrina saluted, and speaking in Galactic, "Ensign Hennesee reporting, Sir."

Commander Ethan acknowledged her with a nod of his head.

When no reply was forthcoming, she asked, "When do I assume

duty?"

"Engineer McPherson will give you the details."

"Thank you." Sabrina turned and went in search of engineer McPherson, whose rank was also that of a commander. She found him in the main engine room. "Commander McPherson, Ensign Hennesee reporting."

"Aye, lass, yer have till tomorrow, five A.M. to come back doon here."

"Thank you, Commander." Sabrina left to find her quarters again. Once settled in, she began to study the tapes Sargon had given her on the Chirons and their language. The Chiron Starship Trefayne, she noted, was not exclusively an interstellar research vessel; if necessary, she could also be used for military deployment.

* * *

When Sabrina awoke the next morning, the bed was warm and the room strange. Naturally, you've landed yourself in another mess, she chided herself. Quickly, she showered, dressed, and looked into the mirror to check if all the creases and pleats of her uniform were in place. Then she ran the brush through her short hair. Before boarding the Trefayne, she had cut her hair again. Suddenly she grinned, remembering the first time she'd worn her hair short. She had been thirteen. Her father had caught her tapping into the computer's phone line to play chess with her friend Hiro, in Japan. As punishment, she had been forbidden to use the computer except for homework or games. Sabrina recalled how angry she'd been, and being rebellious, had cut off her long braids. When she came home, her hair was short, and pink. The first time her father saw her, he laughed so hard he had to sit down. Her mother gave her one look and said, "Not very original, Sabrina." Her aunt Maria Theresa had simply labeled it as being rebellious.

Sabrina sighed. She had won very few arguments where her parents had been concerned. Then her eyes fell on the rank on her collar. She scowled. Heck of a comedown, she thought, for the millionth time.

Checking her timepiece, she had half an hour to get breakfast. Wonder what Chirons eat for breakfast? She soon learned: hot or cold cereal, and juice or hot tea.

When she walked into the mess, it was full, but quiet. McPherson spotted her, and once she had her tray, waved for her to join him.

"Do you have to talk in whispers?" she asked.

Disapproving of her flip remark, McPherson chided her with, "Lass! Noo, that's not too gude a beginin. Did yer have a gude night's sleep?"

"I did. Now tell me what's demanded. It's been a long time since I've been an ensign."

McPherson suppressed a grin, knowing all about Sabrina and the other three. Unknown to her, for a while, as a young boy, he had been on the Antares before Sargon had sent him to Madras, a planet in the Hyades, to learn about engineering.

"Weel lass," he said, ignoring the gripe, "yeh 'come doon' to engineering and I'll show ye the ropes." McPherson patted her arm, then rose and left.

She liked his Scottish burr, but thought it was something more of an affectation on his part. As she sat eating, she wondered why the Chirons didn't object to having McPherson on board. Had he developed a mind-shield? Or is their PSI ability a smoke screen? She lowered her own shield just a little and started to listen with her mind's ear. Amazed, she stopped in mid-bite. No mind-babble! Incredible! Most people, when not actively engaged, allow their minds to wander. As her PSI ability increased, she learned to screen out the bits and pieces of surfaced remembrances or imaginary conversations most people engaged in. But here, the usual thought-jumble was totally absent. The Chirons had very disciplined minds.

As she finished shoveling the last bite into her mouth, she had the eerie feeling that everyone in the mess had at some point begun to look at her. Sorry, she thought, and closed her shield down. Damn! Of course they would notice. They didn't appreciate her intruding into their privacy any more than she did. Red-faced, she swiftly rose. Putting her tray into the receptacle, she left.

When she arrived in engineering, McPherson called her aside. "Sabrina, what were you trying to do?" he asked her censoriously, without the Scottish burr.

She knew what he was alluding to and tried to distract him by asking, "I wonder, do you have PSI abilities?"

"Lass, don't ever do that again."

"I wish I were home," she said, playing with the collar, now showing her lowly rank.

"Aye, Lass, but this is the Trefayne."

"Do you have PSI abilities?"

"No. The Captain showed me on how to discipline my mind so I don't broadcast."

"I see. Just asking, now, what do you want me to do?"

* * *

Duty did not demand much of Sabrina's expertise or tax her brain. It made her feel pretty useless. Her chores were easy, routine, and boring. She knew she was only appended to the engineering department as extra baggage and sometimes made to feel so by everyone, except McPherson. He was the only one who made her feel welcome, and seemed to enjoy her company. The more she got to know him, the more she liked him. When they were off duty, he sometimes let her practice the Chiron language with him.

Initially, McPherson had thought to instruct Sabrina on engineering, but soon learned that she was as knowledgeable as he. She worked well with everyone in his department and never shirked assignments, no matter how tedious.

One day, after leaving the mess, Sabrina decided to visit the rec room for the first time. Usually, after her shift, she went to her cabin and busied herself with the language tapes. The Chirons, while being courteous, never seemed eager to avail themselves of her company. She wasn't actually shunned, just politely ignored. When she came through the door of the rec room, she noticed McPherson sitting by himself, intently studying the chessboard in front of him. She walked up behind him and studied the board.

"Someone has painted himself into a corner," she said teasingly, speaking English. "You always play by yourself?"

Startled, McPherson looked up. "No, not very often. Captain Estel was called away, so I guess I'll have to put these chess pieces up," he mumbled, disappointedly.

"Well," she said slowly, resting her hands on the back of his chair, "Do you mind playing with me? Time goes by much faster when you have something to do, don't you think?"

"You know how to play?"

"Oh, a little. A friend of mine tried to teach it to me years ago."

"Weel, Lass, yer better than noobody."

"Weel," she said, mimicking him, "that's just what I thought." She suppressed a grin as she sat down. She had learned chess from her father, a chess master, and once upon a time, frequently played with Hiro, her Japanese friend, via the Internet.

"Which do you want, white or black?" he asked, lining up the chess board again.

"Doesn't matter."

"Okay, you're white, and you lead off."

At first, just to feel him out, Sabrina played as if she was inexperienced. She lost the first game. The second game, McPherson, perhaps overconfident and a little too inattentive, lost. At the start of the third game she became serious. The tempo of the first two games had been fast and simple. This game moved slowly. McPherson she noticed had to think out every move. Sabrina appeared to be two or three moves ahead of him, and they had drawn spectators.

"Lass," McPherson said, rubbing his temples, "I thought yeh didn't 'knoo' how to play this game," he complained, as he peered into her sea-green eyes, now sparkling with mischief.

"Whoever gave you an idea like that?"

McPherson scowled as he focused on the board. He had one more move left and chose to forfeit the game.

Captain Estel had approached unobserved and been watching for some time. When McPherson forfeited, he moved in. "Would you mind a new player?"

Sabrina stretched and studied him for a moment. He was tall, like most Chirons, with gray eyes and light brown hair. Glancing at the time, she conceded, "Sure, one game." She had addressed him as an equal, totally forgetting that she was only an insignificant ensign.

Estel gave her an odd look, but said nothing. Ian had already warned him that she was very nonconventional, and had provided him with a somewhat abbreviated background of his new ensign.

Sabrina studied the board, planning her opening. She led off with a pawn and he countered with the appropriate move. The next piece was her knight. After he made his play, she sat back to study the board, deciding which strategy to use. The game started off briskly, but soon slowed its pace. Several times, Estel hesitated over a piece and contemplated her with his narrowed gray eyes before going back to analyze the board.

Sabrina watched him in silence. The end of the game was a draw. Estel rose, and with a short nod, left.

"Hmm, dour and silent," Sabrina said in English. "What do you make of it?"

"You'll get used to it," McPherson assured her.

After that, when McPherson wasn't available, Captain Estel began inviting Sabrina to play chess at his personal table in the rec room.

Chapter 2

"Routine, routine, routine," Sabrina mumbled discontentedly. She had been on the Trefayne for six months, and very little of consequence had happened. It left her with too much idle time to think. When she was busy, it was easy to suppress thoughts about Acheron. It rankled. Her emotions were still raw, having only partially succeeded in putting the memory of Machir Aram and the rape into the back of her mind.

"What yer sayin, lass?" Commander McPherson asked, having heard the grumbling.

"It's nice working with you."

"That's what I thought yer said."

Suddenly red alert sounded throughout the ship. In the engine room, for at least five seconds, there was absolute silence. Everyone was poised, awaiting orders from the bridge. When they came, it was to drop energy to quarter impulse power.

McPherson reacted swiftly, but a moment later everything was atilt. Sabrina, almost sliding off her chair, just caught herself. The gravity field began cutting in and out.

The com came on, "Commander Ethan to the bridge; McPherson adjust gravity."

"Sabrina, adjust the gravity generators," McPherson ordered. The floor leveled itself as the gravity field cut in again.

Sabrina shot a questioning glance at McPherson, but he only shrugged. He had no more of an idea what was going on than she did.

She felt like pacing. It was not to her liking to be in the engine room, and foremost, not being part of what was going on up on the bridge.

"Sabrina, cut your emotions! You're disturbing the rest of my crew here," McPherson scolded.

"Sorry, I forgot about that."

Unexpectedly, the ship shuddered. Sabrina recognized it as the effect of an energy torpedo being launched. She half-turned to look over her shoulder just as the whole room began to crackle with static electricity. Wires were burning, and several consoles exploded. One of the young ensign's hands was slightly burned, and McPherson received a nasty jolt.

Suddenly there was an energy fluctuation to the deflector shields. Sabrina literally threw herself across the room to turn off the energy, while at the same time yelled for McPherson.

Before McPherson could see what Sabrina had done, the intercom from the bridge came on. "McPherson, what's going on? We lost our deflectors. Bring up power to the deflectors."

"Belay that order," Sabrina cut in, and hit the lieutenant's hand away from the console, while slamming down on the override.

"McPherson," came Sabrina's terse command, "check the flux in the converter tubes, now!"

"Lordy, lord," came McPherson's agitated remark. "Sabrina, shut off all the non-essential systems."

"Already done."

"Then lass, get me my tools and let's recalibrate that energy flow."

They worked silently together, precisely adjusting the energy flow that powered the Trefayne's engines.

"Now, let's pull out the burned circuits and get replacements," McPherson said, wiping the perspiration from his brow as he looked around. "Lieutenant Norac!" He spoke sharply to the Chiron who was still stunned from being struck by Sabrina. Chirons were not accustomed to being touched, much less hit.

"Yes, Sir?"

"Get replacements for those circuits, and make it fast."

Norac had only taken a step when the doors to the turbo lift opened, and Captain Estel came into the engineering section.

"McPherson, status report, and why was my order countermanded?"

"Sorry, Sir, I had your order belayed," Sabrina told him.

He gave Sabrina a cursory glance, before turning back to McPherson.

"Sir, there was an interruption to the main power current. Had the order been carried out, there would have been extensive damage throughout the engine room. We adjusted the instability in the energy flow, and the power should be up once the circuit panels are snapped in place," McPherson told him.

Captain Estel considered McPherson's statement. His eyes darted to Sabrina then back to his engineer. "Understood, McPherson. Carry on."

"Would you mind telling me what we hit?" Sabrina asked, before he was out of the engine room.

Astonishment registered in the Captain's eyes. The tone of the question was that of an equal to an equal. He considered her for a moment, before replying, "We hit an energy field." He then turned to leave again.

"And the torpedo?"

"Hit a buoy."

"You ran into a space distortion?"

"Yes, apparently, that what it was."

"Was the buoy surrounded by a static energy field?"

"That is what the science officer reported it to be."

"Could I see the computer read-out, later on?"

"You have knowledge of what it may have been?"

"It could have been a transfer point," Sabrina said, more to herself than to Captain Estel.

"Explain that." Captain Estel demanded, sharply.

"You need to contact Captain Thalon of the Explorer. He can tell you more about this. He has encountered a field like this, but only the tail end. There was an abnormal energy reading. When he investigated, he saw the buoy self-destruct. He recorded the phenomenon, and I think he would be very interested in comparing his recording with yours."

"You may view the recording at a later date," the Captain said curtly, then left the Engine room.

Chapter 3

The hum of the engines was hypnotic, almost lulling Sabrina to sleep. Boredom will be the end of me yet, she thought fretfully. Since McPherson and Commander Ethan were off duty, there was not much happening. Lieutenant Norac sat watching the readout on a panel and adjusted a few dials. Sabrina just finished working with her language translator, programming in the Altruscan's language she thought might come in handy some day. Contemplating on how to get Lieutenant Norac's compliance, she absentmindedly put the translator back into her shirt pocket.

Norac, a very young Chiron and only recently promoted, was not too sure of himself where Sabrina was concerned. She did not follow the behavioral script ascribed to an ensign.

"Lieutenant Norac!" Sabrina spoke sharply to get his attention. He turned slowly toward her, his eyes still glued to the monitor. "Since there is not much going on, do you mind if I go up to the bridge? I'd like to view the recordings made of the disturbance we had."

"You're on duty."

"I know, but I will only be on the bridge. I think you can handle anything that might come up," she said with a toothy grin, buttering up the ego of an impressionable young man.

Norac looked at her, then, nodded. "You may go, but, before going off duty, report back to me."

On the bridge, the science officer Commander Somar was off duty.

His relief, Lieutenant Tamar, manned the station.

"May I take the station?" Sabrina asked her.

At first there was no response. Then, with a bored expression she looked up from manicuring her nails, and asked, "Do you have authorization to use the computer?"

"Captain Estel has given me permission to view the recordings made of the phenomenon we experienced recently," Sabrina offered.

"I received no orders for you to use the computer. You will have to wait until Commander Somar returns," Tamar replied, and then resumed filing her nails.

Sabrina, standing behind her, surreptitiously scanned the computer readout coming in. It showed nothing more interesting than the energy reading and noise background of normal space. Biding her time, Sabrina waited until Tamar turned to hand the borrowed nail tool to her friend at the communication center. Instantly, Sabrina's fingers played swiftly over the keyboard. The computer emitted a drawn out screeching noise, and the screen went wild.

Lieutenant Tamar spun around and stared, first at the screen, and then at Sabrina. "What have you done?" she demanded.

"Want me to fix it?" Sabrina asked, solicitously.

"No. Just tell me what you did to it," she retorted, visibly angry.

"Well, that would take a long time to explain," Sabrina said, scratching the top of her head," But if you would let me…"

The doors of the turbo lift opened and Captain Estel stepped onto the bridge. To Sabrina's utter amazement, he was followed by Sargon, Miranda Vindilicii, and Commodore Doeros.

"Lieutenant Tamar, cut that infernal noise," the Captain ordered.

Tamar's fingers flew over the keyboard, but the noise continued. She turned to Estel, "I tried, Captain, Sir," she said flustered, and lost her composure as much as a Chiron could lose such a thing.

Sargon noted how Sabrina stood, leaning lazily against Tamar's seat, daring him to interfere. He walked over to the science station and pushed a single button. Everything went back to normal.

"Spoilsport," Sabrina whispered to him in English.

"What was it?" Estel asked Sargon.

"Oh, only one of Ensign Hennesee's temperamental flare-ups. She has done this type of thing before."

Estel's eyes widened a fraction, showing a touch of amusement. "You seem to know her quite well."

"Oh yes, quite well," Sargon said, with a long-suffering look aimed at Sabrina; his mouth twitched to suppress a grin.

Before Estel could comment or dismiss her, Sabrina turned toward Commodore Doeros. "Ah," she said, her voice cutting, "It is you I want to talk to."

"Yes, Ensign?" he asked brusquely, omitting her name. His brow looked like a thundercloud. He disliked being inopportuned by insignificant people.

Sabrina read him loud and clear. Realizing his opposition, she froze him out with the sheer force of her personality. Totally ignoring Sargon, she locked eyes with Doeros and said, "I want to talk to you about my position on the Trefayne as an ensign. My rank is that of a commander or captain. I am qualified to be a captain, science officer, or chief engineer. If you check my status with Captain Thalon, you will find that I'm overqualified at my present position." Then she looked at Sargon, "This has gone on long enough," she said in a stinging voice. Turning back to Commodore Doeros, "Since the Trefayne's engineering section has a complete crew, I will resign. If you would like to obtain my services at a future time, I suggest you update my file. Captain Thalon could be of some help to you."

She turned to Miranda and asked in English, "You have your ship here?"

"Yes, I came in the Peregrine. Thalon is here with the Explorer."

"I see." Still ignoring Sargon, she asked with a whimsical expression, "Miri, do you need a copilot or a kitchen slave?" With her peripheral vision, Sabrina perceived that Sargon had been caught off guard, and his eyes blazed at her, livid with rage. She had managed to embarrass him by creating a scene, thus allowing Doeros an opportunity to ask more questions about the status of the Antares. Doeros had been pressing Sargon for an explanation as to why the Antareans had yet to assume their duty by joining the Alliance's fleet.

Miranda, aware of Sargon's predicament, shifted the focus back to Sabrina by asking her solicitously, "Bored?"

"Out of my gourd," Sabrina told her in English, and rolled her eyes toward the ceiling. She told Miri about the Trefayne running into a space distortion and the destruction of the buoy. "I know Thalon has investigated these reported incidences and noted that they seem to be getting more numerous. I came up here to view a recording made by the science officer during the Trefayne's approach and the subsequent action. Are you interested?"

"Would you mind running it off onto a disc?"

"Okay, can do." She dislodged Lieutenant Tamar from her seat and in a few seconds handed Miri the disc.

Before leaving the bridge, Sabrina turned to Sargon. "Where are you off to?" she asked it in her most dulcet voice.

He saw no point in showing how infuriated he was by her antics. She already knew that. She would just see what other buttons she could push to get his goat, so he responded, purposely, even-tempered, "I'm going to Ganymede."

Her face lit up. "Are you going to see Kamila?" she asked, delighted.

"Among other things."

"Have you seen the others?"

"Yes. I've seen Sarah and Ayhlean."

"My, you've been busy," she said. When he didn't respond, she took a closer look at his face. There was a puckering around the corners of his eyes and she wondered what amused him. "When you see any of them, give them my love, and let them know how much they're missed."

She and Miri were about to leave the bridge when the doors to the turbo lift opened and McPherson stood at its threshold.

"Jimmy me boy!" Ian suddenly shouted, and swiftly strode in.

Sargon's eyes lit up, and he laughed at McPherson's old way of addressing him. Both men embraced, and in Earth-fashion, pounded each other on the back.

"Jimmy? Me boy?" Sabrina said to Miri, her eyebrows arching. "Wow, I haven't heard that one before!"

Sabrina approached both men and looked at McPherson. For the first time she addressed him by his first name. "Ian, where do you know Jim Thalon from?"

"Oh, I kinda saved his life, and we became friends, then he took me up to his ship," Ian told her. Turning to Sargon, "Did you ever find a name for her?"

"The girls did. She's called Antares."

"Not a bad a name for a ship, I must say."

"Will you quit side tracking," Sabrina complained. "When was he on the Antares?" she asked Sargon.

"During the time you were."

"How come I never met him?"

"I had enough annoyances with you. I didn't wish Ian to be subjected to all the troubles you generated."

"I didn't know you could be so softhearted," Sabrina remarked, affecting astonishment. "But then, he's a male," she added and shrugged.

"You have been too long on Acheron, my Dear."

Sabrina gave Sargon a long look, but chose to ignore the 'dear' and turned back to McPherson, arching her eyebrow.

"To become an engineer," McPherson told her, "Jim took me to Madras to get my degree. So I wasn't that long on the Antares."

"Ah well, I guess I can't win them all," Sabrina said breezily and followed Miri. They entered the turbo lift to go to the transporter room. From there, they where to beam over to Miri's ship, the Peregrine.

The last thing Sabrina heard before the doors closed completely behind her was McPherson asking, "Is she always that bad?"

She could well imagine Sargon's reply.

Chapter 4

Sabrina's body was jarred by a heavy thud, and for an instant she was unable to catch her breath. Cautiously, she moved her head, and the pain made her wince. She found herself stretched out in deep yellow grass with purple tinged hills rising up before her. Stars were visible overhead; it seemed to be close to sunrise. Then, she noticed a boy standing over her and she tried to focus on him. But oh, what a headache! Slowly, she raised herself into a sitting position.

"Are you hurt?" he asked, concerned.

Sabrina activated her language translator, and to her surprise, the boy's speech translated into Galactic after she had him repeat the question, then said, "Yes."

"I am sorry. I did not mean to hurt you. I only wanted the pretty ship to play with."

It sounded reasonable that a child should want something to play with, but she had no idea what ship he was talking about. Again, she forced her eyes to focus on him. He seemed to be nine or ten years old, dressed up as a warrior, wearing a helmet of smooth hardened leather and a small sword strapped to his side.

She shook her head to clear her mind. Nothing made sense. The last thing she remembered was beaming over to the Peregrine. When she arrived this far in her memory, she stood up to look around. This was no ship; she was on a planet. Although her head pounded, she remembered something else: intense pain, and the flaring of blue-white lightning around her. Somehow, something had brought her here.

The boy watched her as though he knew what was going on in her head. "I bet you are wondering how you came to be here?" he asked.

"Yes, it has crossed my mind," Sabrina told him.

"I used my father's magic."

"Magic?"

"Yes. My father still has magic," he said importantly. Then with a secretive tone to his voice, "It's forbidden to use it, but he still does. I have watched him many times make things appear and disappear."

"So you made me appear?"

"No. I just wanted the pretty ship, but now I don't know where it went."

"Where is your father?"

"He is in the tower where the bright sunbeam is housed," he said, pointing behind Sabrina.

Sabrina turned and could see a tower rising sharp and pointed into the sky, its peak divided into two spires with antenna-like projections at their tips. At that moment, two riders came from between two ridges, riding swiftly on horses. As they came near, Sabrina could see that one was a woman, the other a man.

"Who are they?" she asked the boy.

There was a sharp hiss from the boy as he cringed and pulled up his shoulders. "Those are my parents," he said with a quavering voice, "and I'm in a lot of trouble."

Sabrina gave him a sympathetic glance, then, turned to meet the riders. As they came closer, she could discern a worried look on the woman's pale face, but the man was livid with rage.

Sabrina felt the boy move closer, almost hiding behind her. When the riders came near enough to distinguish her clothes, the man's face turned as white as a sheet. Sabrina still wore the uniform from the Trefayne. He exchanged glances with his companion, then, slid off his horse.

"Ninian, what have you done? Where did this lady come from?"

"The magic beam. It was an accident. I only wanted the pretty ship to play with."

He strode toward the boy with his fists raised, "I've told you once; I have told you thousands times…"

"Raban, please," the woman pleaded, and quickly put herself between the boy and him. "He's just a child, plea..."

"I'm not a child!" Ninian screeched, jumping up and down in frustration. "You always treat me like a baby. I'm not a baby. I'm ten years old."

Suddenly there was the beat of galloping hoofs, and Raban turned to look. He shouted to the woman as he jumped on his horse. Bending down, he swept his son into the saddle and galloped away.

Before the woman could set her horse in motion, Sabrina swung up behind her and grabbed the reins out of her hands. She turned the horse and followed the man at a fast clip. They were crossing a valley when cries and the blare of a horn could be heard. An arrow whistled past Sabrina's head, and she let out a yell.

Their path led down into a fold in the foothills, and a vale spread before them. Sabrina could see they were heading toward a fortress built midway up a nearby hill. Riding up to the gate, it opened into a cobblestoned courtyard. When she heard the gate shut loudly behind them, it left her with an ominous feeling, like being trapped. Sabrina guided the horse to one side and as far away from the people as possible. She helped the woman dismount, then, watched her joining her husband.

Trying to keep as much as possible out of sight, Sabrina used the horse to hide what surely would be considered outlandish clothing. These people's dress, Sabrina thought, remembering paintings in museums, must be medieval. From behind the horse, she scrutinized their faces, and especially watched how the lord of the manor was greeted. She saw fear and caution in everyone's demeanor.

At some point she was finally able to catch Ninian's eye and beckoned him.

"Ninian, I need you to help me. I have to get away from here before the people see me. It might get you into more trouble if they saw me. Can you tell me how to get to the tower? Could you show me the way?"

"I don't know if my father will let me."

"We don't have time to ask him right now, as you can see. But you know, you have to fix the thing you did. I can help get you out of the trouble you're in," she coaxed.

"Could you?" Ninian asked, hopefully.

Sabrina hated to mislead the boy, but she knew she had to get away from here. Also, somehow she had to find out what happened to Miri and her ship. She answered the boy as firmly as she could. "Yes, I think I can help all of us, even your father. Because, if these people see me, they will surely make difficulties for him."

"Do you think it will be all right?"

"Yes Ninian. I have to get back to where I came from, don't you see?"

Ninian could see that, and nodded.

Slowly they walked with the horse farther away from the people before Sabrina remounted. Nudging a stirrup out to Ninian, she pulled him up behind her into the saddle and rode away as quietly as she could. Ninian guided Sabrina to a side-door that had yet to be bolted. Sabrina guessed it was an oversight. She let Ninian down to open the door and then helped him to remount. Once outside, she galloped toward the tower, an octagon with a broad base tapering toward the top. It was built on an immense ledge of rock.

After she helped Ninian down, Sabrina dismounted and released the horse. The entrance to the tower was a heavy door. Ninian leaned into it and pushed with all his might.

"Let me help you," Sabrina told him. As they stepped inside, light came on automatically. The first visible object was a thick wooden ladder leaning against the wall, leading from the first floor to the second. Taken by surprise, she stared at the incongruous sight. Electricity and a wooden ladder, she thought.

"Wait a minute," she told Ninian, as he rushed to climb the first rung.

Sabrina noticed writing on the opposite wall and went to read it. A breathy whistle escaped her as she deciphered it, it said elevator. The writing was Altruscan, a language Sargon made sure she studied. He always maintained that it was advantageous to understand your enemy's speech. After Sabrina pressed the up button, the car came down. When the door opened, Ninian cried out in surprise. Obviously, he had never seen it before. Sabrina beckoned him to enter.

When the car started to move, to Sabrina's amusement, Ninian reached with both hands for the floor. She chuckled, reassuring him he was safe. When the door opened on the top floor, it was Sabrina who let out an exclamation of surprise. The room they entered was definitely part of a control tower. She went around the room studying the layout and ran her fingers over the keyboards. "How do I coax the information I need from you?" she inquired of the computer. She began looking for the system console and the housing of the main computer. She found them in the next room with a quick reference guide. "Must be my lucky day," she mumbled aloud as she went back into the control room. She bent over the console and scanned the controls, translating quickly. She turned to beckon Ninian, but he was standing right behind her, looking over her shoulder.

"What did you do when you tried to get the pretty ship?" she asked him.

"This picture was on," he said, pointing to a large screen. "Then I turned this wheel to make the top of the tower move. When the horn pointed directly at the ship, I pushed this button…but the ship disappeared. And when I looked out of that window, I saw you down there in the grass."

"I see," she told Ninian, then sat down at the main console.

To Ninian's delight, she activated the screen. "Are you going to get the pretty ship?" he asked, hopping from one foot to the other.

"First, I have to find it. I have to find out where the beam sent it." Sabrina's fingers danced over the keyboard, activating the view screen and scanners. She set the scanners at their widest range. Amazingly, she had a signal. After she enlarged it on the screen, there was a faint blip. As she watched, she realized that it was heading away. In frustration she ran her fingers through her short hair. "Damn, Miri, how am I going to get your attention?"

In desperation, she sent out an SOS, the old Earth distress signal. Sabrina boosted the signal three times, but there was no response. The blip vanished from the screen. Nevertheless, she continued sending the signal. Suddenly, an alarm shrieked, "Intruder alert! Intruder alert!"

It made Sabrina jump, and she quickly switched the sensors to scan inside the tower. A sole life form was coming up in an elevator, and Sabrina surmised, to the top floor where the controls where.

A new sound made Sabrina spin around in her chair, and she stood up. There was a second elevator. As its doors opened, Ninian's father stood crouched between the doors.

Sabrina watched his stealthy movements as he entered the room. Then saw a glimmer. In a split second, she recognized the shining silver of a knife. Immediately, she pivoted backwards on the balls of her feet, and with a well honed reflex, snatched the knife out of the air. She grabbed Ninian and held him firmly, the knife pointing at his throat. But Raban only laughed.

"I have more sons, and this one is of no importance to me," he told her as he slowly stepped farther into the control room. He quickly brandished another weapon that looked a lot like a gun. Sabrina released the boy and pushed him to the floor. Throwing the knife, she hit Raban mid-chest and he went down. She watched him for a second, listening to his labored breathing, then cautiously moved closer to get the weapon.

As she bent over him, his hand shot out and grabbed her ankle before she could jump clear, throwing her off balance. She fell, but the moment she hit the floor, she rolled and leaped to her feet. She whirled around and hit him with a quick jab to the throat. He let out a choking gasp.

This time, she double checked before getting near him. After she got the weapon, she took a closer look at his him. He was at least part Altruscan. At some point, she became aware of the boy moving cautiously to stand beside her.

"Is he dead?" Ninian asked in a hushed voice.

"I'm sorry. Yes. He's dead."

"I'm not sorry. He was mean. He was always mean to my mother and me. I'm glad he is dead." He sniffled and wiped his nose on his sleeve. Clenching his hands into fists, he tried very hard to be brave. But the stress was too much for him. On impulse, he flung himself into Sabrina's arms and cried.

Sabrina cradled him and soothingly stroked his head.

The computer cut in with another intruder alert. Again she set the scanner to search the inside of the tower. It registered one life-form. Watching closely, Sabrina decided that whoever it was didn't know about the elevators: it was climbing the ladder.

Ninian tugged at her sleeve, "I think this is my mother," he told her.

"Probably so. Let's go see."

They entered the elevator, and the car descended to the second floor. After the doors opened, they could see a woman trying to pull the ladder up after her. Ninian immediately ran out shouting, "Mother, Mother, I'm here. I'm here."

She let out a gasp and turning around, dropped the ladder. She knelt down and embraced her son and began to cry as she gathered him into her arms. When she saw Sabrina, she shrank against the wall.

"Where is Raban?" she asked in a whisper, her face white and her eyes wide with fear.

"He's dead," Sabrina told her bluntly.

The woman slid to the floor and huddled against the wall. "What do you want with us?" she asked, apprehensively.

"Nothing," Sabrina told her. "If you want, you can come with me."

You are not Altruscan?"

"No."

"She's a nice lady, and she's going to find the pretty ship again. Let's go upstairs," Ninian said. Squirming out of her hold, he impatiently pulled her by the hand. "Come on Mother. It's all right."

She rose slowly and let Ninian lead her toward the elevator. Hesitantly she entered the lift behind Sabrina. When the elevator started to rise, Ninian's mother had a shocked expression on her face. When the boy laughed, the fearful look disappeared.

In the control room, Sabrina programmed the sensors to scan space again. To her relief, the blip was back and much larger. She cut off the automatic S.O.S. and opened a hailing frequency, hoping for an answer from Miri. Still, there was only static. She sent another burst of the S.O.S. and received a Morse code signal telling her to "Continue transmission so I can home in on it."

Suddenly, Ninian gave a shout. "Look, the pretty ship is back! Look at it Mother. Oh, look at it."

Sabrina switched to scan the inside of the Peregrine and watched as the image became clearer. Slowly, a picture materialized. Surprised, Sabrina looked at it. Although it showed an individual, she couldn't make out if it was male or female. The figure was gaunt; the facial features could belong to either gender. Sabrina opened hailing frequency. "Are you receiving me?" she asked in English.

"Yes, very clearly," a husky voice answered in the same language. "Hey, you're not Miri!"

"Neither are you."

"You must be Sabrina."

"Yes. Where is Miri, and who are you?"

"I'm Lara Ensor, a friend of Miri's. Who is that with you?"

Sabrina turned toward the woman, holding the translator toward her. "What's your name, and who are you?"

"I'm Thea; I was Raban's hostage, not his wife. My father is the Doge of Ravena. Raban demanded me as a hostage. I was his security against my father's people. In return, he promised not to use the lightening from the tower. But he used it anyway. Many people, especially those who opposed him, disappeared."

"Who was Raban?" Lara asked.

"As far as I know, he was part Altruscan. There was a struggle for power within his own organization, and he prevailed. He signed a peace treaty with my father and I became the collateral against my people."

Sabrina's face softened, and she asked, "How did the Altruscans gain control over your world?"

"History says, that when their first ship appeared, the Altruscans were thought to be saviors. A plague swept periodically through most of our populated areas, and many people died. The sickness didn't seem to affect the Altruscans and they gave us medicine. When the first ship left, they promised to return with more medical help." Thea paused for a moment.

"When they returned," she continued, "we received them with open arms. Slowly they took control over everything, even over our private lives. It started with groups of young boys disappearing. Soon after, the boys were openly rounded up and herded into their ships never to be seen again." Thea's voice faltered and grew husky, her eyes watered. "We were turned into slaves; we were forced to grow food for them; we had to strip our land of most of its ore and minerals. Then one day their supply ships quit coming, and from that time on we tried to regain our world. It was a long war. Finally we arrived at a truce and I was demanded as a hostage."

As she listened to Thea, Sabrina remembered Sargon once saying that no one should suffer the tyranny wielded by the Altruscans.

Lara broke into her reverie. "Sabrina, do you know you have a reception committee outside the tower?"

"I do? Well, let's see what they want?" Sabrina turned to Thea, "You think you could talk to them?"

"Of course."

Sabrina turned the sensors toward the outside of the tower. "Do you recognize any of these people?" she asked Thea.

Thea took a closer look. "Yes, that one is my father's adjutant, and the others are some of his top ranking officers."

"Will you and Ninian be safe with them?"

"I think so."

"I can't force you, but I think it's best if you left the tower and went away with your people."

"What will you do?" Thea asked, apprehensively.

"Lara," Sabrina said turning to the screen, "is there anything you want to do here?"

"I think there are records that could be of interest."

"I see what you mean. You're going to beam down here?"

"I think your friend should leave with her people, first."

Thea looked anxiously at Sabrina.

Sabrina handed Thea the microphone. "Don't tell your people about Lara and me. We will stay for a while and shut down the tower so it can't be used again. Only tell them that Raban is dead and you and your son are coming out."

"What will I tell them about how Raban died?"

"Tell them he fell down a deep shaft. Hold the microphone like so and push this button to speak."

Thea drew a long breath, contemplating Sabrina, then, nodded her head. "This is Thea," she said. "Raban is dead. Ninian and I will be coming out."

"Short and to the point. You did well," Sabrina told her. "Go into the elevator. I will set it for the first floor and open the tower door for you. She bent down to Ninian, "Can you keep a secret?" When he nodded, Sabrina continued, "You can never tell anybody about the pretty ship; it must remain a secret. And… nobody needs to know how Raban died. Can you do that? Keep this very important secret?"

Ninian looked at her, "I can't play with the ship?"

"No Ninian, it's not a toy. It's a very big ship. It only looks small on the picture screen because it's far away. You will understand better when you get older." Turning to his mother, she said, "Thea, you need to go now, or your people will get restless and wonder what's going on up here."

Sabrina turned the translator off and put it back into her shirt pocket as Thea and Ninian entered the elevator. Sabrina set it to go down. When Thea and her son reached the first floor, Sabrina opened the tower door and watched as they walk out. Thea was immediately surrounded by her people and plied with questions.

"Close the door, girl," a voice said sharply behind her.

Sabrina spun around. The woman standing behind her was tall and gaunt, her skin slightly blue and her hair a brilliant red mane. She had tawny eyes.

"Do I pass inspection?"

"Miri sure has interesting friends..."

"Sabrina, quick, shut the door," Lara interrupted. Turning back to the screen she saw Thea's people moving to enter the tower. Sabrina slammed the door on them.

"So, you're Sabrina. Have you any idea where Miri is?"

"Nope."

"Tell me what happened."

"Well, I was to beam across. Miri said she was coming over in her own way. She told me she didn't like to have her molecules disassembled. The last thing I remember was searing pain and a flash of blue light. Next, I was lying on the ground. When I looked up, a little boy asked where his pretty ship had gone to," Sabrina said with a grin. Then asked more seriously, "I imagine you have searched for Miri?"

"I contacted the Trefayne," Lara answered, "but they only knew that Miri had left, and that you were also gone. Thalon said that he would mind-search for Miri, so I decided to follow the curious ion trail that brought me here. I'm glad I did; at least I've found you." She stepped towards the panels, and continued. "Let's get busy downloading all the data stored in these computers. Then, we'll shut this place down. After that's done, we'll go and see if Thalon had any luck finding Miri"

Chapter 5

Back on the Trefayne, Lara docked the Peregrine in the shuttle-bay. A mechanical voice from a loudspeaker told them to report to the briefing room. When they entered the room, Sabrina got an icy stare from all those assembled.

"Curious," Lara said, turning back to look at Sabrina, "I swear it just turned awful cold in here."

"Zero Kelvin," Sabrina told her, dead-pan.

Lara responded with an amused flicker in her amber eyes.

Not one individual at the conference table seemed in the least amused, but there was a chuckle, and a smooth, black-haired head with a pronounced widow's peak rose from behind a console screen.

"Miri!" Sabrina exclaimed and continued in English, "Where on Sam's hill did you disappear to?"

"Dunno. Though I met an old man and had a long conversation with him."

"You don't mean God?"

"I don't think that's who he was. He wasn't omniscient. He didn't know me, and he had no idea how I got there."

"Well, that's a relief. Can't have you floating around on a cloud, playing a harp."

"Fat chance; it's too damp and drafty on a cloud."

Commodore Doeros, ignoring Sabrina, turned to Lara. "You have some information for us?" he asked with chill civility.

"Yes Sir. Sabrina, would you please run the first data disk."

Sabrina bit her lip and sent Doeros a scathing look, thinking you pompous ass, as she inserted the disk. It first showed an aerial view of the tower, and then the control room. Also, Raban's body.

"Who is this?" Sargon asked in Galactic.

"His name was Raban. He was part Altruscan."

"Anything else?"

"No, Captain Thalon," Sabrina said, keeping her face expressionless. "Anything else would be conjecture. Lara and I down-loaded the computer information and erased all its memory, then shut down the tower. There was an underground entrance and we destroyed that. Last, we locked every egress we could find."

Doeros listened impassively while inspecting the palm of his right hand. Again ignoring Sabrina, he asked Lara, "With how many people did you interact?"

It was Sabrina who answered. "Only a small boy and his mother. It was the boy who interfered with the transporter beam. He used his father's magic because he wanted the pretty ship to play with."

Not disposed to decipher Sabrina's cryptic remarks, Doeros again ignored her. "Commander Ensor and Commander Vindilicii, you can continue with your exploration. We will access the data you have given us." Doeros not amused by Sabrina's glib attitude, forced the words out, muffled between his teeth.

Lara and Miri straightened up, turned smartly, and marched out. Sabrina, disregarding protocol, sauntered out behind them. When she found her duffle bag inside the door of the Peregrine, a thin smile cracked her lips. Sargon, she knew, had taken time to tell someone to have her things packed.

The three boarded the Peregrine and left the Trefayne.

* * *

After clearing the Trefayne's shuttle-bay, the Peregrine returned to the course previously locked into its guidance system.

"Sabrina, you have galley duty," Miri told her.

When Sabrina only answered with, "Aye, Sir," and promptly left, Lara looked a little surprised.

Miri laughed. "Don't be deceived by the performance you've

witnessed. She's good at giving orders, as well as carrying them out. She's a damned good science officer and engineer. Also, she's a better cook than you or I."

"Then you like her?"

"You didn't get to know her?"

"Not really. She seems to be a wit with her jokes, though."

"Oh that's just a façade she irritates certain people she doesn't like, you know, Doeros."

"Well, he's a pompous ass, most of the time."

"As far as I'm concerned, he asked for it."

"She wasn't too nice to Thalon either. She completely ignored him."

"Ya, I noticed. Nevertheless, he's proud of her."

Miri only got a "humph" from Lara.

"Let's lay in a search grid, and see what we can come up with."

Somewhat later, the ship's air became filled with a delicious aroma.

Lara looked up from her station. "I agree. You were right. Let's see what she's cooked up."

Miri set the Peregrine on auto-pilot and they both went to the galley. When Miri opened the door, Sabrina was just setting the dishes on the table.

"I think we are right on time," Lara said to Miri, and to Sabrina, "It smells good."

Without looking up, Sabrina said. "Sorry about planting myself on you two. I hope you don't feel you're stuck with me."

"What would you have us do? Jettison you out into space?" Miri asked.

"Well… you could drop me off on the Antares."

"Fat chance, we are light years from the Antares."

Sabrina's mouth twitched. She knew that.

In spite of herself, Miri laughed, and Sabrina breathed easier. She knew, for all her easy-going manner she wouldn't care to tangle with Miri. She surmised that Miri, as well as Lara, could be formidable adversaries.

"What have you planned?" Sabrina asked.

"We haven't figured out a strategy yet, but we have put in a search grid," Lara told her.

"I've thought about this for some time. A buoy disappeared on me once when I was on a science outing with Thalon. If we back-track, provided you two have a record of the earlier appearances, we could find out where they went, instead of where they came from," Sabrina said.

"That's not a bad idea. Maybe I could reconcile myself to you coming along," Lara told her.

"It was nice the last time she tagged along and we netted the Altruscans' weapon arsenal."

Sabrina quickly turned away to hide her grin.

After eating dinner, all three returned to the cockpit and Sabrina activated the computer screen. Miri handed her several data disks, and then for a while, the silence was only broken by comments pertaining to the data on screen. They scanned back to all the previous appearances. What emerged was an anomaly in space that centered around one planet. The appearance of the disturbances seems to be recurring at definite intervals.

"Let's see what interest this planet holds," Lara suggested.

Miri laid in the course. "All right, warp six."

* * *

Within four hours, they reached their destination. From space the planet resembled a blue-green ball with white floating clouds. There were several continents, and in the southern hemisphere a great storm was brewing. There were no energy readings which would indicate an advanced industrial society. The ground, visible from space, was mostly laid out in agricultural patterns. They only detected small towns and villages. At the northern hemisphere, a short mountain range grew out of the grassland with one tabletop mountain standing all by itself. When they passed over the mesa, the sensors picked up some very curious readings.

"Look at these readings! What do you make of it?" Miri asked Lara.

"It's definitely odd, since we only get it when we pass over the one mountain. Perhaps, it's where they land with their ship."

"Possibly. Sabrina, what kind of energy do you think it is?"

"Beats me." I've never ran across anything like it."

"Think we should land?" Miri asked Lara.

"Yes, that's our best bet, but after the sun goes down. Let's circumnavigate the planet and collect more readings to be sure this is the only place. Let's scan for life-forms."

After a space of silence, Lara asked Sabrina, "What did you get?"

"Only a small settlement near the mesa and a lake." Topography shows that we could easily approach after dark and set down within the mountain range, close to that mesa."

"Sounds good." Lara said, then after glancing at the chronometer added, "You take first shift, Sabrina. Miri and I'll sleep, then, Miri will relieve you in about four hours.

* * *

After entering the planet's atmosphere, and as soon as the Peregrine hit air, it sprouted wings. The view screen automatically went up, and was replaced by windows. Leaning over Lara's shoulders, Sabrina checked the coordinates, and Miri piloted the Peregrine, now turned aircraft. She settled it down in a depression halfway up the mountain nearest the mesa. Before the craft shut down, the Peregrine's wings retracted.

The time was just before dawn when the door at the side of the Peregrine opened, and the three women, dressed in camouflage uniforms and wearing utility belts, came slowly down the steps. Halfway down, Lara took a deep breath and immediately wrinkled her nose. Lifting her chin, she sniffed. "Do you smell that?" she asked Miri. The air held a sweet, cloying scent.

"Yes, I smell it too," Miri said, after taking a whiff of air herself. "There's some sort of overriding scent. Sabrina, do you get it?"

"Yes, it's from a plant with tiny blue flowers. Thalon once collected the leaves for medicinal use. It's called a…damn; I don't remember his ever telling me what it's called. It's analogous to cannabis with similar chemical properties. The leaves have to be harvested before the blooms fall off, or it converts its potency to seed production."

"Could that be a piece of the puzzle?" Lara asked.

"You mean the plant?" Miri responded back.

Lara shrugged. "That or something else the planet has to offer."

Before Sabrina was all the way down the steps, Miri had already moved on to survey a large tree. Sabrina scrunched her face and complained, "Surely, you are not going tree climbing again?" On their previous adventure, Miri and Sabrina had found themselves in a jungle and the trees with their interlacing branches had made a usable highway.

"Quit your act. I got your number a long time ago," Miri said, wagging a finger at her. "What have you got against trees? Of course, if you don't want to, you don't have to."

"Yeah, right, and me miss out on all the fun."

"Whatever makes you happy." Miri laughed then pulled herself up into the tree. Lara and Sabrina followed suit. Seated on their perches, they began scanning the area through high-powered binoculars. It gave them a detailed view of the valley. The inhabitants of the small village seemed to be still asleep; nothing stirred, not even the wind.

"Look there," Lara pointed," up that slope; see the vines? They're cultivated. What are those?"

"Grape vines?" Miri suggested.

"No," Sabrina told her, after adjusting her binoculars. "Those are the plants we smelled. Curious, I've never seen them cultivated. I assumed they only grew wild."

After another period of silent watching, Lara exclaimed, "I think we're finally getting our first glimpse of the inhabitants!"

The village was beginning to stir. One door after another opened and the people came out. Animals were turned out to graze, and smoke began to rise from the chimneys. Soon the whole village came alive with people going about their business. The men and women were dressed in similar brown, gray or bluish pajama-type jackets and trousers.

After sitting in their observation tree for a while longer, the three decided to set up rotating shifts watching the village. Miri and Sabrina left, leaving Lara straddling a branch and leaning comfortably against the tree's trunk.

* * *

Sabrina had just taken over the watch from Lara when she noticed several villagers balancing huge baskets on their heads. They where heading toward the cultivated plants and began to harvest the leaves.

Adjusting her binoculars, she focused in on the people, and a gasp escaped her. There were a couple of people with cancerous growths covering large areas of their faces. Several had little or no hair, and there was a small child, a dwarf, stumbling along on crippled feet.

Sabrina swung out of the tree and headed toward Miri. "Hey!" she called softly. When Miri turned, she said, "I think we have some kind of radiation poisoning here. We need to find out how prevalent it is. I've just seen several people with skin cancer, a deformed little girl, and quite a few others with little or no hair. I don't like what I'm seeing."

Miri squinted at her. "Don't you think you're jumping to conclusions?"

"No Miri, I don't think so. There was an accident some time back on Earth; a reactor meltdown. Those are the types of symptoms shown on old broadcasts about radiation sickness and later genetic damage. I am really concerned about this."

"Okay, as soon as it is safe, we will beam over and check out the area."

After the villagers had gone back into their homes for their evening meals, Miri beamed Lara and Sabrina across to the lone mountain, then commenced following them in her own way. They materialized on top of the mesa, attired in protective clothing.

Sabrina took a sensor scan. "Miri, look at those readings."

"Damn. Lara, what do you make of this?"

"I hope the whole mountain isn't hot. Look at those blackened rocks. Looks like thruster burns. Their ships, whatever the type, are leaking atomic radiation. Either, they are primitive, or very careless," Lara said.

"I told you the people I saw showed exposure to radiation," Sabrina said. "Let's check how much of this mountain is contaminated."

They split up and worked their way down. The hottest area was confined to the top of the mesa. The radiation, albeit getting weaker, was nevertheless detected all the way to the mesa's base.

After gathering outside the Peregrine, Sabrina asked, "What's on the agenda now?"

"Mostly, we wait and see, "Miri told her.

"Wait until we discover who's visiting here at those very predictable intervals," Lara remarked, while stripping her outer clothing and putting it into a bag. She entered the Peregrine wearing only her bare skin and headed straight for the shower to decontaminate.

* * *

Several days later, after awakening from a nap, Sabrina stepped outside and found Lara gone. Strolling over to Miri who was seated in a chair under a tree, reading a book, Sabrina asked, "Has something happened? Where is Lara?"

"No, nothing happened. Lara is just being Lara," Miri informed her. "She went off to a tarn she discovered, and I guess she went swimming."

Sabrina scowled. "She could have invited us."

"Nope, she wouldn't do that. Don't get in Lara's way."

"What do you mean by that?"

"Just do as I say. Lara has her own ways. She's not like you. She is not even like me."

"Very interesting my dear Holmes, but would you explain this to a slower Watson?"

Miri laughed. "So you read Sherlock Holms. Sabrina, some day, maybe, I'll explain some things to you."

Suddenly, somewhere in the distance, there was the baaing of sheep. A little later Lara appeared over the ridge in the midst of a flock of sheep with the shepherdess.

"Did she make friends with the shepherdess or the sheep?" Sabrina quipped.

"More likely with the sheep," Miri told her, deadpan.

By then, sheep, Lara, and the shepherdess arrived.

"Miri, do you think you could communicate with her?" Lara asked.

"Well, let's see." Miri brought out her translator and spoke to the shepherdess, pointing to the sheep, and the village in the valley, but the translator was unable to render anything intelligible from the girl's responses.

Sabrina, standing off to one side, gently probed the young girl's mind. Transmitting the question mind to mind, she then repeated her question into the translator.

"Yes," the girl answered in her language, "I am from the village."

"What happened on that mountain?" Sabrina asked telepathically, then, spoke the question.

"The gods came from the sky in their chariot," she told Sabrina.

"What do they want?"

"The palapa leaves."

"Have people been sick since the god's came from the sky?"

"Yes, the gods have punished some people with sickness."

"Do you serve these gods, gladly?"

"No, they force us to serve them."

"When are the gods coming back?"

"Soon, because we have harvested most of the leaves."

"Would your people wish to leave the village?"

"Yes. But we are forbidden to do so."

"Your name is Ana?"

"Yes."

"Then, Ana, you need to tell your people to pack everything they can carry and leave here now, never to come back. The mountain the gods have touched is taboo, never to be approached, not in many, many, many lifetimes."

Sabrina hesitated while studying the girl's reaction. "We will talk to these gods and they will never come back. Now, please go. Tell your people they must leave before the gods return." Sabrina smiled at the girl, and motioned for her to go.

After the shepherdess left, Sabrina turned to Miri, "You think the translator has picked up enough to decipher her language?"

"I'm working on it," Miri answered and turned to Sabrina, "I think you did it."

Chapter 6

After the villagers left, there was stillness over the land, almost a waiting hush. Sabrina never remembered what first drew her attention toward the sky on this calm, clear morning. There was brightness growing, and getting intense.

In the cockpit, Miri was playing a computer game with Lara, while keeping an eye on the monitors. "Hey Lara, there was a blip. You think I should power up the Peregrine? Why don't you go and asked Sabrina."

Lara only shrugged, and walked outside. She sat down next to Sabrina and told her, "We got a blip, and Miri wants to know if she should power up the Peregrine."

"Not yet," Sabrina told Miri over the communicator bracelet the three kept at all times on their wrists. Then, pointing to the sky, "You see that? I have been keeping a watch on that shimmering glow." Then, of a sudden there was a dazzling flash across the sky. A brightly burning object entered the atmosphere and a faint roar grew steadily louder.

Miri, now leaning against the doorframe of the Peregrine, watched with Sabrina and Lara as the object executed a flip and turned into a sleek, shiny, flame-spouting rocket. It began a slow descent onto the mesa. Suddenly, the thrusters shut off and with a thud, the rocket settled down on its fins. Minutes passed, then, a door slid open, releasing stairs to the ground and an individual, muffled in a space suit stepped out and looked around.

Miri's listening device soon picked up two voices; to her surprise, they spoke a language that translated into Galactic.

One astonished voice said, "They are not here."

"What do you mean they are not here?"

"Just as I said. There is no one here."

"Where could they have gone?"

"You think we should check the village?"

Miri quickly went back inside the Peregrine. Soon, her voice sounded over the loudspeaker she had placed days earlier, close to the landing site. "No, you will go nowhere; you have already contaminated this area with radiation. Who are you and where do you come from?"

"Who do you think you are, asking us these questions?"

"I am a representative of the Planetary Alliance," Miri told them. "Again, I ask you to leave, and I repeat, you have already contaminated this area and its people."

"They have an herb we need to counteract radiation sickness."

"We know. The palapa leaves, as the natives call them. If you needed help, why didn't you contact the Planetary Alliance, instead of frightening primitive people? You are some interesting gods, I must say," she added, derisively. After a short pause, "Do you want us to intercede with the Alliance for you?"

The individual turned toward the opening in his ship. Apparently, there was a short whispered conference, then he responded with, "The answer is no. We will go back to where we came from. No need to bother others people with our problems. It would only cause interference into our affairs."

"Suit yourself," Miri told him. "The thing I strongly emphasize is do not come back. We will be monitoring for your tell-tale space distortion, and you will be prevented from invading any Alliance Space."

It only took a short time for their rocket to fire up. When it gained enough power, it lifted off. After reaching altitude, the rocket-ship moved toward the buoy in space. As soon as it entered the distortion, the buoy destructed.

"Well," Sabrina said cheerfully," now we can leave here and go back home."

Lara looked at Sabrina, then, abruptly walked away.

Surprised, Sabrina went toward Miri who was just exiting the ship.

"Hey, Miri, what's with Lara? We are leaving, aren't we?"

"What happened?"

"I told Lara that since we are finished, we could leave, and she just stalked off."

Miri chuckled. "Come here; I think we need to have our talk. Let me begin by saying that Lara is Lara. She is not explainable. Not even by me. Come let's sit in the cockpit."

After they were settled, Sabrina asked, "What and who is she, then?"

"I'm sure you tried to mind-touch her, like you did me."

"Oh, so you noticed."

When they first met, Sabrina tried to mind-touch Miri and had gotten a complete shut out. She had also tried this with Lara. However touching Lara, she had felt something so alien, she recoiled immediately.

"Yes. I noticed. I'm still somewhat human. Lara isn't. So, don't do it again. I may only shut you out. Lara could lash out and you may get hurt. She tolerates me because there is sort of a friendship between us. We have had some experiences together. We survived together."

"I would appreciate if you explained how Lara and you differ. Naturally, I have noted it."

Miri thought for a moment, and then began to chuckle. "I'm sure you remember the story of the mad scientist who toyed with genes, and I told you he was insane."

"Yes. I remember."

As Miri continued, her expression became more serious. Sabrina could feel touches of pain and despair, and yes, also a touch of insanity.

"I will only talk about me. I told you that I came from the same planet as you, Earth, and also how, for the longest time, I tried to piece everything together. I began to remember that I had been married and had children. I now know where I lived and that I loved to walk along a river's embankment. It was where they beamed me up. I felt myself literally dissolving, and when I awoke, I was lying on an operating table. I will never forget the faces of the people who stood around me, probing my insides. For a long time the only memory I had was of excruciating pain. Whoever did the probing didn't care a hoot of what they did to me. Next, I woke up in a cage, literally a cage".

"There was another female there with me. It was Lara. We couldn't communicate. As time passed, partly to maintain our sanity, we began to teach each other our languages. Lara is from the Altair system. One day, men came and took Lara. She was never brought back. I told you about Karsten and how we escaped. We found Lara. She was different, and I still don't know what had been done to her. She doesn't talk about it. I advise you to be very cautious around her. Don't provoke her."

"When we leave here, we have to get food supplies, especially protein, and fresh vegetables. You will meet someone who is like Lara and me. Her name is Cassandra. I don't know how she will take to you. Right now, I am going to talk to Lara. You wait here."

Sabrina was left somewhat dumbfounded by the cryptic tale, which explained nothing. Before Miri could leave, Sabrina put a staying hand on her arm. "Miri, your disappearing trick, that's something you acquired after you left Earth?"

"Yes." Her reply was short and terse.

Once more outside, Sabrina was chewing on a stalk of grass and mulled over what Miri had said. Then, something gelled. The strange feeling she had around Lara, and sometimes Miri, was what she experienced with Serenity the Arachnid. Serenity, an Alliance council member had the same ability to disappear as Miri. However, where Miri could be light-hearted and merry, and Lara at times appeared to have a sense of humor, Serenity felt cold and devoid of emotion. But there seemed to be a commonality, something they had in common.

After a long while, Miri returned with Lara. "Let's get the Peregrine ready for take-off," she told Sabrina.

Chapter 7

Sabrina had just entered the cockpit. Bending over Miri she looked at the view screen. Startled, she took a step back for a better view. "What on Sam's Hill is hat?" she asked.

"That's Cassandra's world."

"Yes, but what is it?"

"I don't know. It reminds me of a tubeworm which lives on the ocean floor. From all I've seen, it doesn't have a mouth and digestive track, and it seems impervious to the cold of space. I suspect it absorbs energy from its surrounding. All I know is that it is alive and growing." More to herself than Sabrina, she continued, "Last time I saw it, it wasn't that big!"

"And Cassandra lives inside of it? Inside this worm?"

"No, not the whole worm. Only the tail end. I don't know anything about the rest of it."

"How does she get water and energy?"

"She has water-makers that remove moisture from the air. Also, she uses Sonofusion for energy. There is some kind of containment that protects the worm."

"Interesting. I heard Thalon…"

"Sabrina, don't get into it. I barely understand how the Peregrine works."

"Okay, I won't," Sabrina placated her as she watched Miri cut the Peregrine's power to glide slowly toward Cassandra's world. It looked as if someone had strung a gigantic tube all over space. There was no discernable pattern. In some places the worm had bulges. Miri set the Peregrine gently on top of one of the smaller bulge. Sabrina became alarmed when the ship began to sink slowly through the material.

Miri giggled. "You had a worried look on your face, Sabrina."

"Well, I'm all for new experiences, but I'd like to be warned beforehand."

"Then, it wouldn't have been a surprise. Remember what I said about Lara's unpredictability? It goes double for Cassandra. So watch your step."

For a second, Sabrina's eyes showed a flicker of disquiet as she gave Miri a fleeting look. Pulling a face, she whispered, "Thanks for the warning."

The Peregrine settled to the floor. Before exiting the ship, Sabrina gave Miri a questioning glance.

"Just stay with me," Miri told her.

"And Lara?"

"She'll join us when she wakes up."

Sabrina followed closely behind Miri through what seemed to be a long tunnel. There was a free floating light-glob overhead, dispensing light, and it seemed to follow them. Soon, they came upon an aperture which slowly retracted, and they entered an anteroom. At the opposite side, a wall made of a permeable membrane, let them pass through.

As they came through the membrane, Sabrina gasped. She had stepped onto a sandy footpath, and beside it ran a small gurgling rivulet over rocks. Nearby were trees and flowering shrubs. Further down was a bench, and at the end of the path were steps leading into a color-filled garden. A pile of rocks at the center of the garden resembled hollowed-out boulders, each one with a large opening in front. Through one of these openings walked a very striking female with lavender skin and blue eyes.

Miri greeted her with an enthusiastic wave of her hand.

"You said you needed Zirbelnuts?" Cassandra asked Miri in Galactic.

"Yes, we need a small supply for the Peregrine and some fresh vegetables. Can you spare some?"

"Yes, I have enough. Who is this?" gesturing at Sabrina.

"Her name is Sabrina. You remember her? She belongs to Thalon."

Cassandra looked at Sabrina with a scowl. Yes, she remembered. Thalon had gotten made at her for playing a prank on the Four while they were on the holo deck. That was a long time ago, but Cassandra still harbored ill feelings. As they slowly moved on, Cassandra, passing under a tree, plucked a pair of fruits, and handed both to Miri.

Miri gave one to Sabrina.

"Miri," Lara called. She stood bare-footed in the rivulet, letting the water splash over her feet, "Do you want to stay here?"

"Maybe for a while," Miri agreed.

With a sudden flare of irritation Cassandra pointed at Sabrina. "She can't stay," she snapped. "She has to go, now."

Sabrina was surprised at the sudden attack. Astonished, she looked at Cassandra and then at Miri. Miri only shrugged, apparently ill at ease.

"She can leave with the other ship," Cassandra added curtly. "I don't need it. She can have it. It's in the other bulge."

Miri tugged at Sabrina's sleeve. "Come," she said, tersely.

While they walked hurriedly back through the tunnel, Sabrina asked, "What's going on?"

"I don't know."

Sabrina, bewildered by the abrupt hostility, had no inkling of how she had incurred Cassandra's wrath. All she had felt from Cassandra was indifference for the most part, as though she hadn't been there. Becoming more apprehensive, Sabrina followed, uncertain of what to expect. Soon, they came to a ballooned out area much like the one they had left the Peregrine. In it stood a small spacecraft; much smaller than Miri's ship.

"Go! Leave! I fear you are in danger," Miri whispered, and shoved Sabrina toward the ship.

Bewildered, she looked at Miri, "From Cassandra?"

"From her, or the worm."

"How so?"

"I don't know, but leave now, please," she warned, then turned sharply and hurriedly left.

When Sabrina moved towards the ship, she saw that the door

was already open. The moment she entered, it closed behind her, and simultaneously, the life support system came on. To Sabrina's consternation the air smelled stale and musty. Dim emergency lights bathed everything in an eerie red glow.

"Computer," Sabrina repeated in several languages as she hurried toward the cockpit. There was no response. She was near panic when she felt movement and immediately guessed the ship was passing through the material of Cassandra's world the same way the Peregrine had entered. She was falling through space. The realization generated a sinking sensation in her stomach. Suddenly she had the distinct feeling that Cassandra was getting even with her, but she knew not why.

Standing in the cockpit, she squinted at the instruments. Unable to read the ideographs, she broke out in a sweat. She let herself sink slowly into the pilot's seat, as she wiped her face on her sleeve. Shaking, she took several deep breaths to calm herself. She was ready to push any key to see what would happen, when she thought of Marathi. She had a rudimentary understanding of the Orion's language.

Why not? she thought, and tried it. "Computer?"

"Working," came the computer's monotone voice, and Sabrina drew an easier breath.

"Translate Marathi to Galactic."

"Commencing," was the reply in Galactic.

"Start engines."

"Engine warm-up initiated."

"How long to engine start?"

"Ten seconds."

"Continue."

When the engine fired, Sabrina almost let out a whoop. At last she had halted the free fall. Next light came on, as well as the viewing screen. The sensors were scanning forward.

According to the computer, she had about twenty-four hours of air left. There was no food or water on board. The computer showed a space station twenty-eight hours away, and a planet forty-five. She laid in the course for the space station and cut the air flow to half-volume. Sitting back, she monitored her breathing so it came slow and even. Also, she cut down on unnecessary movements. Next, she brought up the blue print of the engine, the circuitry, and the layout of the entire ship. It was much smaller than Sabrina first surmised. The ship had one cabin with two bunks and thank God, a head and a shower. Underneath, going along its length, was the ship's hold. Also, in accordance with the ship's diagram, there was a closet with a space suit. And, according to the computer, it was still intact. Sabrina found the closet and the suit, and when she tried it on she found the air to be stale, like in the ship. However, it was enough to last her at least an hour, if she should need it.

After putting on the space suit, she returned to the computer, trying to ignore her growling stomach. She hadn't eaten since Miri handed her the fruit from Cassandra's garden.

Twenty-seven hours later, the ship's air ran out. She closed herself in the space suit, set the air output to halve, and went back to analyze the computer's data. Thirst plagued her now, and she caught herself licking her lips. Also, a lack of sleep was beginning to make her groggy. She began to nod off, feeling dizzy at times and disoriented. When the computer informed her "Space station ahead", she thought she was dreaming. With effort, she pulled herself together. The station's control was asking for identification. Sabrina tried her voice but could only manage a croak.

"Are you in distress? Do you need assistance?" someone from the station asked.

Sabrina sent an emergency signal. Just before she fainted, she felt a tractor beam lock onto the ship. When she regained consciousness, she was lying on a stretcher and a medic bending over her.

"Are you all right? Can you hear me?" he repeatedly asked in Galactic.

She blinked and gave him a wane smile, touching his arm to let him know that she had heard him. When he put the oxygen mask over her face, she took several deep breaths. "I'm okay, I just needed some air," she assured him, but when she tried to sit up, she lost consciousness again.

The next time she awoke, she was in a hospital bed, attached to a contraption dripping fluid into her veins. "Oh God, what a mess," she mumbled.

Chapter 8

Back on the Antares, it was two weeks since Sabrina, Yoshi and the others had left on the expedition.

Ayhlean awoke even before her alarm went off. Usually she was not up at five in the morning. Last night, Erin asked if she would help with the kids in the martial- art class. There were six of them between the age of ten and sixteen, and they become unruly, especially without Yoshi there to keep discipline. Erin and Yoshi had been the oldest of Ayhlean's set of four. Both were now in their twenties, and since Yoshi's absence, it had fallen on Erin to manage the kids' martial-art activity.

Thank God for small favors, Ayhlean thought, relieved that Erin was old enough to take some responsibilities off her shoulders. She still had to teach regular classes and run the Antares. As she slipped into her gym suit, she was surprised when her doorbell chimed. "Come in," she called.

Erin's head appeared first, and when she saw that Ayhlean was ready to go, she breathed a sigh of relief.

"What's going on?" asked Ayhlean.

"Those kids won't listen to me. Ever since Sabrina left, they have been on their worst behavior."

Ayhlean contemplated Erin for a few moments. She knew the kids were only testing their limits in how far they could push her buttons. Sabrina, or Yoshi, had only to walk in, and immediately everyone fell in line.

"You just have to get tough," she told Erin.

"Like Yoshi?" she asked, with a wane smile.

After Yoshi took over from Sabrina it didn't take him long to learn that camaraderie didn't work and followed Sabrina's example, he made them toe the line.

"Yes, just like Yoshi. Let's go and see what's going on."

Arriving at the gym, they walked into bedlam. The kids were running all over the gym, yelling and chasing each another. The noise was deafening. Ayhlean blew her whistle and two kids responded. Two were unaffected by the whistle, and the remaining two were engaged in a fight. Ayhlean marched up to the two boys who were fighting and kicked their feet out from under them. "Twenty push-ups," she ordered. When Mustafa balled his fists, she told him thirty, and for him also to sound off.

He eyed Ayhlean specuiatively. A crooked grin curled his lips as he smirked at her. When he saw he was outnumbered, he decided he better comply and dropped to the floor. Sarah and Kamila had just walked in.

Sarah slipped quietly up behind Erin and startled her. "Having trouble?"

"Yeah," Erin grumbled.

"Edwardo and Mustafa again?"

"Yeah!" Those two are at each other again. Ever since Yoshi left, Mustafa has become a pain."

Both boys were sixteen. Mustafa had belonged to Sarah's set, and now lived in the dorm. As soon as he finished his push-ups, Sarah pinched his earlobe. "Little brother," she said, her voice gentle and reasonable, "if I hear another squawk about you, we're going to do a little work out with a quarter-staff, and if that doesn't help, I won't be loathe to talk to Sargon."

He gave Sarah a sullen look.

"Well?" Sarah said, softly.

"Yes, Sir."

Kamila eyed Edwardo. "That goes for you too, sweetie," she told him. "But I will ask Sargon to spar with you."

Edwardo only sucked in his breath. He knew Kamila. For all her apparent softness, underneath, she was more like unyielding steel.

46

Ayhlean turned to the other kids. "Since you're so full of energy this morning, you will do five laps, double time. Commence."

There were some grunts and groans, but they instantly obeyed.

"See, Erin, that's how it's done," Ayhlean told her.

"You grow up with them, and you think they are your friends and like you enough to make your job easier," Erin groused.

"That's the price of command," Ayhlean told her, and smiling wagged Erin's chin. Then she patted her gently on the cheek, "You will learn."

Exercise took a good hour. The kids left to shower and then go to the cafeteria. Ayhlean and Sarah were still straightening up the gym when Sargon's voice came over the intercom.

"Sarah and Ayhlean, report to the briefing room."

They looked at each other for a second of silence.

"Well, he's still alive," Ayhlean mumbled. Sargon had been absent for a considerable length of time.

"You haven't gotten into trouble yet, have you?" Ayhlean asked Sarah, half-smiling at her,

"Nope."

"Wonder what he's up to?"

"Well, we'll find out when we see him."

Just as they turned to leave, Kamila came rushing back into the gym. Grabbing Ayhlean by the sleeve, "What's going on?" she demanded.

"We'll let you know when we know," Ayhlean told her quickly, then trotted out after Sarah.

When Sargon walked into the briefing room, Sarah and Ayhlean were just sitting down.

"What's up?" Sarah asked, leaning back in her chair.

Sargon eyed them pensively without answering.

"I don't like those long looks," Ayhlean told him.

Sargon laughed. "I'm trying to decide how to spring something on you."

Now worried, the girls looked at each other, and then back at him.

"Spring what on us?" Ayhlean demanded.

Using a rare teasing approach, Sargon said, "A long time ago I decided that as soon as I thought you were ready or…old enough,

I'd throw you out of the nest, and now that time has come." Looking at their shocked faces, he added, more reassuringly, "It's not as bad as it sounds. Ayhlean, since you are interested in administration, there is a position for you with the Quarter Master on the Space Station Sigma IV." Then turning to Sarah, he continued, "And you are going to Madras, a planet in the Hyades. You will have an internship in a hospital there. You will need to pack, but take only what is necessary; the rest of your things will go into storage. Meet me in six hours on the hangar deck."

The three rose simultaneously, but the girls more slowly.

"But, Sargon," came a plaintive voice. When he looked at Sarah, she looked like a frightened child, and Ayhlean suddenly broke into tears. He came around the table and gathered both into his arms. "Come on girls, it is time you met the world."

"But we have never been off the Antares," Sarah reminded him.

"Yes. I know. That's why it's time for you to leave home. I'm not abandoning you. I will keep an eye on you two."

"But Sargon, this is too sudden. What about Sabrina? Could you just wait until she gets back?" Sarah pleaded.

"Maybe you could give us more time to get used to the idea?" Ayhlean added.

"Sarah, love, you know Sabrina won't be back for another three and a half months. And, it's about time you found your own feet. You have six hours. Now go and pack."

Kamila was waiting for them not far from the briefing room. When she saw their reddened eyes and damp faces, her worried question was, "What's going on?" Her eyes moved anxiously from face to face.

"We have six hours and then we have to leave the Antares," Ayhlean informed her, and broke down crying.

"Oh, my God, what is he thinking? What about me?"

Sarah put her arms around Ayhlean as she looked at Kamila. "We don't know. He didn't say anything about you."

"We better go pack like he said and get the Antares ready for turn-over," Ayhlean said to Sarah as she reluctantly disengaged herself from the comfort of her arms.

With the same feeling of foreboding she had experienced when Sabrina left, Kamila watched the two leave, then stalked off to find

Sargon. But like always, he was nowhere to be found, so she went to Ayhlean and helped her pack. After finishing, both went to see about Sarah. They found her sitting dejectedly in her chair, staring through tears at the floor.

"Sarah!"

She looked up. She hadn't heard them come in. She stood up a little stiff and calmly said, "I'm finished packing." There was a catch in her voice, but she shook herself hard. "This is foolish. Let's have a drink. Before Sabrina left, she gave me her apricot brandy. She told me to have one on her, sometime."

She went to get the brandy and the glasses. When she came back, Kamila's face was whet with tears. To Sarah's disapproving look, she said peevishly, "I don't like saying goodbye." There was helplessness and pain in her eyes.

"Kamila!" Ayhlean said a bit sharply.

Kamila frowned at her, "I know. Sorry. I don't like all these changes. I like things to stay the way they are."

Ayhlean wanted to say something soothing, but could think of nothing that would have sounded sincere. Instead, she silently touched Kamila's face and pushed a strand of hair out of her eye.

After sipping from her brandy and licking her lips, Kamila suddenly asked, "Do you remember the pledge we made after Sabrina was gone? Well, is it still on, or not?"

"You mean the one about perpetuating Sargon's genes?" Sarah asked astonished. "It's not going to be easy with us in different parts of this galaxy. What do you want us to do, seduce him before we leave?" she added amused.

Ayhlean giggled.

"No, of course not. Don't be silly. But are we still going to go ahead with it?"

"If it's possible," Ayhlean said, looking wistfully at the other two.

It was something that had been on their minds for a long time, especially Ayhlean's. They talked about it on and off, but, without Sabrina being present. Fearing Sabrina's derision or non-compliance, they had waited until she was gone.

Having a child meant continuity for Ayhlean, someone to remember her when she was gone. It really didn't matter to Kamila if she had a child or not since she came from an Arabic background were children belong to the father and not the mother. Sarah, growing up as an orphan, wasn't too sure if she wanted to raise a child by herself. She only went along because she was sensitive to Ayhlean's need.

* * *

Next morning when Kamila awoke, she knew she was alone. Sarah and Ayhlean were gone. Of the four, she was now the only one left on the Antares. Stretching sensuously, Kamila thought that for once she was going to have it her own way. She began to sleep in late and eat when she felt like it. There were several novels to read, and now that no one was going to make demands on her, there was time to do the things she had always dreamt of doing. So, why wasn't she deliriously happy? She began to prowl the ship and made a big nuisance of herself. She even missed Sabrina.

In the beginning, when they first met, they didn't start off on the best footing. Sargon seemed to treat Sabrina special, and it made her jealous. She considered herself far more feminine and appealing than Sabrina with her tomboyish behavior. Right from the start she was aware that Sargon treated her differently.

To Kamila, special treatment meant special favors. It had been imprinted on her early in life, in Lebanon, where she grew up. It was vitally important to please, if you happened to be female. Observing her mother, she learned how to humor males and their whims. Kamila watched her mother cajole and placate her husband, while sensing her underlying fear. Men had power. Even when she was small, she learned to prattle prettily with her father or grandfather, since pleasing them made live easier.

She tried the same strategy with Sargon, and it seemed to work for her until Sabrina came on board. Sabrina, even at that age, had little patience with Kamila's feminine wiles. Only gradually did it dawn on Kamila that Sargon only humored her because he thought of her as a child. It never entered his mind that she was using feminine subtleties on him. Much later, she realized she had wasted a lot of energy resenting Sabrina. First, she learned that Sabrina did not dislike her. It was only her behavior that annoyed her. Then, being special to Sargon was not an easy life. He had been stricter and more demanding of Sabrina than of the rest of them. Another belated discovery was that Sabrina was a good friend to have.

* * *

Kamila never knew when Sargon returned to the Antares. One morning she walked into the cafeteria and there he was. She slid into the seat beside him and asked, "When did you get back?"

"Why?"

Caught a bit off guard by his brusque reply, she didn't know what to say. Swallowing her pride, she asked, "How are Ayhlean and Sarah doing?"

"I surmise they are doing fine."

"Now I know why Sabrina always gets so exasperated with you."

"Is there something you need, Kamila?"

"No."

"Then I would advise you to find yourself a table."

Stung, and her face crimson, she rose wordlessly and left the cafeteria. Later that afternoon Michael came to her apartment, but only showed his head around the door. "Sargon wants to see you in the briefing room."

"Do you know what he wants?"

"No, he didn't say." he replied.

"Thanks, Michael. I'll see you later."

"You said you were going to have lunch with me. You know you promised."

"I'll see you after I see Sargon. Okay?" When the door closed behind him, she smiled wryly. "I guess I'm next," she said to herself.

Sargon was busy running a program on the computer and curtly waved at her to sit down. When he shut the program down, he looked at her with that appraising look that always portend trouble.

"You will leave tomorrow for Ganymede. In the morning," then he added, "early," as if he knew she had been staying in bed late since the others had been gone. There had been no incentive to get up since she had been relieved of duty. Her job had passed on to the younger set. With an effort, Kamila kept her voice even when she asked, "Is there anything I need to know?"

"Only that Ganymede is a matriarchal society. It should be an interesting experience, coming from an Arabic background. You will join the household of Mahala Tatai; she's a friend of mine. She's the head of a large department at a University. I guess you would call her a dean. She will assign you to an appropriate branch when you get there."

Kamila swallowed, but never found her voice. She left, her steps reluctant, but she felt vastly relieved. It had finally come; the waiting was over. She too had to leave home.

Chapter 9

Ganymede was different, then, it was not so different. The society was separated into two halves, just like the country Kamila had come from. Men and women lived divergent lives. The difference on Ganymede was that the women held the power.

Kamila sat on the outdoor portico of the beautifully pillared house of Mahala Tatai, sipping wine and discussing the difference of their societies. The scent of jasmine and the fragrance of roses mingled in the afternoon sun. Inside the house the lilting voice of a child sang a happy song.

Mahala smiled. "My granddaughter," she said, and then, continuing their conversation, asked, "So, you were saying…things were different in your society?"

"I'm not talking about the Antares where status is accorded to merit, but the country I came from. There, men hold all the power, have all the privileges. Even religion only favors men. Women are chattel. They have no rights, and often no recourse to justice."

"You sound bitter."

"I know: Thalon has remarked on that, too. I remember when I was little, my mother was forced to do things she cared not to do. And I remember her fear, constantly placating an irascible old man, my grandfather. Also, she feared my father who didn't hesitate to beat her if she displeased him."

"Those are harsh conditions," Mahala sympathized, her lips pursed in distaste.

"Yes, but women learn to use stratagems in order to survive."

"In my experience," Mahala said, "women have always been more intelligent where life and living is concerned. Men are very primitive. They only long for earthly pleasures. Even their gods are endowed with human attributes. Men invented gods of war, gods of justice, and so on. Even their heaven is fashioned after earthly delights. On the other hand, women like order, but also beauty, and the stability of a home where children can grow up in safety. My observation is that women are more practical and down to earth."

"But, are your men happy with this arrangement?"

"We don't ask them if they are happy, just that they are obedient and follow the rules laid out for them."

"But what use do your men have besides the obvious?"

Mahala laughed at her. "Kamila, we don't waste talents. We screen them early to discover their aptitudes and then educated accordingly. There are many men who hold important positions on Ganymede."

Kamila nodded as she digested this interesting piece of information. "I don't think that Thalon would fit into that scenario," Kamila said, musing, then broke into an amused smile.

Mahala threw her head back and laughed. "No, Kamila, I don't think so, either. He is a law unto himself."

"You talk like you know him well?"

Mahala managed a bland face, saying, "We became friends," thinking of the many nights, when both being young, had spend in each others arms.

* * *

Kamila was overjoyed when Mahala informed her that Thalon was on Ganymede and would stop by to see her this afternoon. She was watching eagerly for him, and when she saw him walking along the lakeshore, ran toward him with outstretched arms.

Sargon chuckled and accepted her embrace.

Impulsively she said, "I missed you, Jim," and then turned crimson. The name had slipped out, and at that moment, she realized just how much she had missed him.

She knew he was distancing himself when he responded, "I have been apprised of your many accomplishments since you arrived."

Shaking an accusing finger at him, "You checked up on me."

"No. Everyone I met is telling me how much they like you, and how well you've adjusted."

"I see." Putting her arm through his, she led him up the path and through the garden to her bungalow. "Come inside. It's a little cooler."

The room was large and furnished a little too opulent for Sargon's taste. But then, Kamila had always liked comfort. She chose to live in a bungalow along the lakeshore rather than in the dorms. She enjoyed the quiet and privacy, never really having had it before. Pointing to a comfortable chair, she said, "Why don't you sit down? I just fixed some iced tea. Would you like some?"

Before he could answer, she was already in the kitchen, and he could hear the clinking of ice. Coming back into the living-room, she handed him a glass and continued their conversation. "It's nice here, and I like Mahala. I do enjoy my work and the people."

"But how well have you adjusted?" he asked, taking a careful sip. The tea was good and not too sweet.

"Without much difficulty," she said nonchalantly, sitting down in the opposite chair. "But this society really is a change. From the Antares as well as the one I came from. Here, the women are the heads of their households. And they hold all the property. But what really surprised me was the segregation of the men. The boys are separated from their families when they reach fourteen. Then they have to live in houses and areas just for men. Not until they are chosen by a woman, can they join a family again. At least, the women treat their men with consideration and let them develop their talents, or whatever gifts they have."

Suddenly her mood turned somber as she looked at Sargon and her voice became bitter. "At least they're not treated like chattel."

"It still rankles, after all these years?"

"I mostly remember my father never taking me seriously, like I didn't matter."

"That is why I chose Ganymede for you, so you could experience another way of life."

"Well, I understand all that, and it's nice and good, but when can I go home? I have so many ideas and experiments I'd like to try on the

Antares. There is a wide variety of plants I would like to introduce."

"Not for a while, Little One. Have you found nothing to keep you here?" He looked wistfully at her. He had hoped she would find someone to love.

Studying Sargon, Kamila knew very well what he had on his mind. There were some men she found interesting, but she had never seriously consider it.

"Don't you want us to come home?"

Sargon smiled. "Yes, someday."

"Someday can mean a long time."

Again he smiled. "You still need to stay here."

Kamila gave him a long look, but decided to skip a confrontation, for the time being. "You know, I have learned quite a bit about horticulture and botany. And you know, I have even become interested in genetics. Not only plant genetics, but human genetics as well. It's interesting how much one can do with bio-engineering. The women here are doing a lot with chromosome splicing."

Sargon nodded. "They have eradicated most of the genetically transmitted diseases and deformities. And they have worked a miracle on a planet called Acheron."

"Isn't Acheron where Sabrina is?" Kamila asked.

"Yes."

"How is she doing?"

"She's doing well," Sargon replied.

Setting her glass down, Kamila said, "I don't mean to change the subject, but, how long will you be here?"

"Three days." He checked his watch, "And right now, I need to go to meet Mahala." He rose, and she followed him to the door.

"Three days, should be time enough," she mumbled loudly enough to intrigue him.

It had been loud enough. Being curious, Sargon half turned and asked, "Time enough for what?"

"Well Sargon, you and I need to have a very serious discussion."

"About what?"

"I'll tell you if you come this evening. We could have dinner together. Might that be convenient?"

Sargon looked at her with a puzzled expression. He sensed conflicting emotions from her. His curiosity was aroused, but he couldn't stay. "I have a business appointment with the Women's Council and Mahala is sponsoring me, so not tonight," he told her. "But I can see you tomorrow."

"Then, until tomorrow," she agreed. Leaning against the door post she watched as he walked away.

* * *

Kamila was nervous. She fussed over the table, rearranging the setting and flowers for the umpteenth time. Then, she plopped herself down on the couch, hugging one of the pillows. Of all the damned chances, it had to fall on me to put the plan into motion, she thought, feeling glum as well as uptight. She couldn't stand the inactivity for long and jumped off the couch to pace from the living room to the kitchen and back again. She was forever checking the food.

Stopping outside the kitchen doorway, she scratched her head, musing. "How in the hell do I get Sargon to go to bed with me? I never seduced a man in my whole life," she said aloud. It had fallen to her to implement the plan she, Sarah, and Ayhlean agreed on before leaving the Antares.

When Sargon came that evening, despite all her worries, she had dinner ready. She informed her curious friends that she would be entertaining a special dinner guest and would appreciate no interruptions.

His first comment upon entering her bungalow was, "You did a lot of mental pacing."

"I wish you wouldn't read my mind. I have been nervous. This is the first time I prepared a meal for a guest, and I want it to be perfect."

"First, Little One, I don't read people's minds. Second, the table looks very nice; thank you for the effort."

Kamila handed him a glass of wine and was still watching for any reactions in him. She was dressed in a colorful floor-length gown and wearing a perfume her off-world friends assured her would seduce any man. They didn't know Sargon. He did compliment her on her dress, and she noted signs of a response to her perfume.

At first, their conversation around her elegant candle-lit dinner table was small talk. She asked what he knew of the others, where they were and what they had been doing. As the dinner progressed, Sargon's curiosity grew. She had made a point about needing to talk to him, but as far as he could tell, she had yet to address anything he considered significant.

Kamila guided the conversation slowly into her botanical endeavors. "I have been working on rescuing a rare specimen of giant conifers that is dying out here." She drew a breath, stole a look at Sargon to gauge his interest, and continued, "For germination, they need the conflagration of a fire to open the seed pods. Really, the loss of this species would and could affect a whole eco-system."

Sargon, patiently listened and still wondered where all this was leading to.

Then she went on to describe the different human races she had encountered since coming to Ganymede. "I never imagined there could be so many different colors, sizes, and shapes to people. You know," she finally said, "I never met anyone looking like you."

"I don't think you ever will," Sargon told her smiling. There was a nagging suspicion growing at the back of his mind. But Kamila wasn't Sabrina. He didn't expect any deviousness from her.

She finally came out with a full attack. "Don't you think it would be a shame to have something so rare lost to posterity?"

Slowly he turned his face to her. "What?" Sargon stared at her with open astonishment.

"Sargon, you are an idiot. Don't you want to have children? All of us, Ayhlean, Sarah, and I would gladly bear you a child. We know you refuse to choose between us, but at least let us have something that is part of you."

"Who put you up to this?" Sargon exploded.

She took a deep breath. "No one put-me-up to this," she minced out the words. "We all decided, and I think Sabrina will concur, if it's presented to her in the right way."

"You must be dreaming if you think Sabrina will agree to this."

"I don't give a damn whether Sabrina agrees to it or not," Kamila said, heatedly.

Sargon threw his head back and laughed. "Little One," he addressed her with deliberate patience, "I think she would have a lot to say about it."

"Will you stop calling me Little One. I'm more than thirty years old, and I consider myself a grown woman. I think you still see us the same way we were when you found us. Sorry, we-are- no- longer-children. And, I am serious about my proposal. We think you owe us this much."

Sargon suddenly stopped laughing. "Kamila, I brought you here where you have the opportunity to find a mate, someone to love. I can't go to bed with any of you; don't..."

Kamila suddenly jumped up and exploded with her fist balled in front of her, and went on the offensive. "Do you consider yourself too good for us? Are we nothing but an experiment to you? Are you laughing at us? Do you think we're foolish for even considering the enormity of wanting a child from you? Have I overreached myself, my Lord." When she called him my lord, she used Sabrina's intonation of voice, and made a deep obeisance.

Sargon at first looked nonplussed, then, became serious. "Kamila, you cannot in all seriousness believe a thing like this. You can never know what all of you mean to me. To think such a thing is unfair."

"Then, why- don't- you- do- as- I- ask? We have taken a blood sample from you." When Sargon nearly rose from his chair, she waived him off with, "We know that you can father children with aliens like us. Is this idea so distasteful to you?"

Sargon looked at her, shaking his head, and there was an explosive expulsion of breath. Inhaling deeply, he asked, calmly, "Was this dinner and perfume to seduce me?"

"Absolutely."

"Kamila, my child, there is nothing distasteful about you. Any man would be happy to have you. I simply have never allowed myself to think of you girls in this manner."

"Does that mean you are backing out? Is that your way of letting me down?"

"I need time to think about this."

"Oh no, I wont give you that time."

Sargon looked at her. He was amused, and he was also touched. He loved her because she was Kamila, as he loved the others for that particular something that made up their personalities. But this! In truth, he knew there had been times he had considered the possibility of having children by the Four.

Suppressing a grin, he said in his most peremptory manner "Come here." When she stopped beside his chair, he pulled her into his lap. "Is that better?" he asked.

"This could be a beginning," she said, and as she looked up at him the corners of her mouth pulled upwards.

"This is your first time, isn't it?"

"Yes. I was going to have your child or stay a virgin for the rest of my life."

"Was this going to be a threat?"

"It was next on my agenda if you didn't agree."

"I see."

When Sargon kissed her, his kisses were gentle at first and then became more passionate. When she had a chance to come up for a breath, she said, "You're no virgin."

"Whatever gave you that idea?"

"Well, how could we have known? We thought maybe you took an oath of celibacy."

"Not very likely."

After making love to him, Kamila nearly drifted off to sleep when she thought of something. "Sargon, you know, the others will be very mad at you for denying us all this time."

"Are you telling me you had pleasure?"

Her only response was a murmured "mmm" as she pulled him close.

* * *

On their last morning together, Sargon had accomplished what he set out to do on Ganymede. The counsel renewed his agricultural contract, and something he never dreamt of. He lay in bed with an almost feline sense of abandon and well-being, watching Kamila go about her morning toilette.

"Now that I finally have you, you're leaving me," Kamila said with mock despair.

"I'll be back."

"That's what they all say," she mumbled.

"What did you say?" He had heard her.

"That's nice."

"That's what I thought you meant."

Before he left, she gave him a letter for either Sarah or Ayhlean.

He came back three more times, and when she knew she was pregnant, she rejoiced. When her child was born, Sargon was with her, easing her through labor. It was a girl, and she named her Soraja. She had Sargon's eyes. Kamila and Soraja stayed four more years on Ganymede before returning to the Antares.

Chapter 10

After Sargon left Ganymede, the Explorer stopped on Sigma IV for a layover to re-supply the ship. Since this would take some time, he handed out passes for his crew to enjoy themselves. Getting through signing several requisition sheets, and concluding other business, he checked the personnel roster to see where Ayhlean was on the Space Station.

When Sargon walked into Ayhlean's office, the Staff Sergeant was in the process of running a program. He held up a hand and pointed to a seat, saying, "I'll be with you in a sec."

Sargon, suppressing a grin, waited patiently for his reaction when he looked up.

When he did, his face fell. Rising with alacrity, he came to attention. "Sorry Sir. I apologize."

"It's all right. I get busy like this sometimes, too."

"What can I help you with, Sir?"

"Is Lieutenant Thalon in her office?" he asked.

"No Sir, she's in a staff meeting. She won't be finished for another half hour. If you wish, I could page her."

"No, it's not that important."

"After the meeting, she usually goes to the officer's mess."

"Thank you Sergeant. I'll find her."

An hour later, when he walked into the mess, Ayhlean stood with several officers in a corner of the room, holding a lively discussion.

Sargon walked quietly up and stood behind her. As he listened in, he realized it was an argument about a new program that had come in that morning, down from the top.

"It won't work," she argued, "I tried it. It makes more of a mess than clarifies the issue."

"Lieutenant, I don't think you have enough experience to doubt your betters," she was told.

"Aw..."

"Put a sock in it," Sargon finished for her in English.

Ayhlean spun around "Jim!" she exclaimed, then came to attention and saluted.

"Aw, cut the bunk," Sargon told her, using one of Sarah's favorite expressions.

"Yes Sir, immediately," Ayhlean said and laughed.

"I'm hungry. Do you think we could sit down somewhere?"

"Yes Sir." Turning to the other officers she excused herself with, "Later, I will explain to you why it doesn't work." She walked off with Sargon, knowing there were some sneering looks behind her back. Ayhlean chuckled. "They don't like my high-handed approach."

"Well, Lieutenants have to mind their place," he teased her.

"Lieutenant, indeed," she said with some acidity. On the Antares she held the hard earned rank of Commander.

After they had their trays, "Now tell me, where did you come from? How long will you be here, and where are the others?"

"Tall order before I even have the first bite in my mouth."

For a while she let him eat in silence. "Well?"

"I have been on Ganymede."

She searched his face. But lacking Sabrina's abilities, he easily hid his feelings from her.

"Then you have seen Kamila? How is she?"

"She is fine." Sargon was toying with her. He knew what she wanted to know. He was curious too how ingenious she would be in approaching the topic.

"I had a letter from her, and she told me she was interested in genetics now."

"Yes. I am very pleased in her choices for expanding her knowledge. She is studying bio-engineering." Sargon said matter-of-factly.

"How long will you be here?"

"At least several days."

That's enough time, she thought. "Do you have a place to stay?"

"Not yet."

"You could stay with me."

"I don't think so."

Ayhlean was getting frustrated. Something in his demeanor told her that he was reading her like on open book. He knows. Of course he knows. She hoped Kamila did break the ice. What she didn't know was how to approach this subject. She felt shy and clumsy. It was easier to work out a scenario in her head than to apply it in reality.

"Sargon."

"Yes, Ayhlean."

Oh, damn you, she thought. How in the hell am I supposed to manage this?

Sargon, being less ethical, read her mind and enjoyed her predicament.

"I think there is something we need to talk about. Maybe tonight, when I'm off duty? Around seven. At my place."

"Where are your quarters?"

"On level five, cabin fifty-six."

"Okay, I will see you then."

* * *

At seven her doorbell chimed. When she opened the door, Sargon stood at its threshold proffering a bundle of flowers.

"My, my, my," Ayhlean said in her best Sabrina imitation.

Sargon grinned. "I've been told never to arrive empty-handed at a lady's door."

Ayhlean smiled up at him, her eyes bright, shining with happiness. "Come in. I'll have dinner ready in a minute." She took the flowers and went in search of a vase, then set it down on the elegant dinner table. After she served the food and they had eaten, Sargon smiling and feigning innocent curiosity, asked, "What was it you wanted to discuss?"

"Before we left the Antares, there was a decision Sarah, Kamila and I made concerning something that is vital to us. It needs to be taken care of. It absolutely needs to be done."

"Yes, I am listening," Sargon answered.

"Last time we were together, we talked about the uniqueness of some beings. You know the ones there are few in this universe."

"What are you getting at?"

"There are people in this world…" Ayhlean suddenly expelled a heavy breath. "You can be the most uncooperative, stubborn…" She stopped in frustration, not knowing how to continue. "You know, I like to throw this vase at you. I'm trying to seduce you, and that's something you didn't teach us. You have been very remiss on that subject."

Sargon leaned back in his chair, pretending to be confused. "I thought we were having a nice, pleasant dinner together, and now it's turning into a heated philosophical discussion?"

"You said you were on Ganymede. Didn't you have a talk with Kamila?"

"Yes, we talked. We discussed biology and her new interest in bio-engineering."

"Then you did talk about biology?"

"Of course, it is a very interesting subject."

Ayhlean suddenly caught a flicker of a smile. "I believe you're pulling my leg. I bet you talked about reproduction to Kamila. Am I correct?"

"We talked about genetics."

"Ah. There it is. Genes. More specifically, yours?"

"Yes, she happened to mention something about that too."

"Now, would you talk to me?"

"About what?"

"Oh, for heaven's sake, Jim."

Sargon pursed his lips to suppress his smile. "Oh I see. What you are getting at is my biology, and yes, we talked about that and reproduction."

"Then, will you agree? You don't have to say I do or anything like that," she assured him, her words tumbling almost breathlessly from her lips. There were tears in her eyes. "Sargon, all I want is a baby from you." And then with a whimsical smile, "It would be a shame if your genes should be lost."

"There you go, bringing up genetics again. Ayhlean, did it ever occur to any of you that someday I may want to marry someone?"

Ayhlean's hands flew to her mouth, and she stared at him. "No, I never thought of it. You mean you have someone else in mind. Have we been presumptuous? I'm sorry. It just never occurred to me. I'm sorry if I embarrassed you," she stammered. Ayhlean was mortified. She had taken for granted that it would always be like it had been, Sargon and the four of them.

Sargon watched her for some time, and waited for her to calm down. When he rose, she jumped up from her chair. She was sure he was leaving her. But he walked up to her, and enfolded her in his arms. She broke into tears and he held her tightly until she stopped crying.

"Ayhlean, I have been with Kamila, and she is pregnant."

Not believing what she was hearing, she was speechless. Then, she expelled a long, heavy sigh. "She is?" she asked, her eyes slowly lifting up to see his face. And then, in utter amazement, she saw the amused look. "You did? Oh Jim, I'm so happy for her," and her arms went around his neck. "Please, for me. You know how much I want to have a baby."

"Well, after opening this can of worms, I guess I have to go through with it."

"What do you mean by a can of worms?" Ayhlean asked, incensed.

"How are we going to explain this to Sabrina?" Sargon asked.

"Oh, her, you just leave Sabrina to me."

Only before he was leaving did Sargon give her Kamila's letter. He intently watched her face. At first she looked perplexed. Then she read it a second time. When she gave the letter back to Sargon, her face had turned serious. The letter read:

Dear Sarah and Ayhlean,

To put it bluntly, it has fallen to me to break the ice. I have conceived; I am carrying Sargon's child.

However, this is not the purpose of this letter. I don't know if you are aware that I'm living on Ganymede, which is a matriarchal society. Some of their ways of life I like. It's much easier for women than for men. But this is also not the sole purpose of my writing.

I would like to propose something which grew out of Sargon's reluctance to father a child with us. Here on Ganymede, everyone belongs to a house. Belonging to a house means belonging to the family. You, Sarah and I have adopted the name Thalon. So we could consider that we belong to the house of Thalon. Now back to Sargon's reluctance. We could ordain a rule such as this:

Any male of a house who is not bound by a promise to a woman-- is not related by blood or marriage to a member of the house-- has the obligation to father a child, if so asked.

I know this is not in a legal form; it's only an idea I had. If you agree, please send it on to the others. We could call it house rights. How does that grab you?

Kamila.

"Will you agree if this becomes a... let's call it, a rule? Have you thought about the implications?" Sargon asked, after reading the letter, still amused by his girls' contrivance. He decided never again to underestimate Kamila, as he handed the letter back to Ayhlean.

She hesitated, holding the letter suspended in the air, thinking for a moment. "I don't know, Jim," she said slowly and thoughtfully. "It needs to be seen if we can agree to such a far-reaching idea. We four, I think, will need to discuss it when we meet again."

Chapter 11

Sabrina, after being released from the hospital, thought to find out what kind of accommodations a Space Station offered before looking to see if Ayhlean was still stationed here. However, the first thing on her agenda was to find a restaurant or some kind of eating place. She had enough of the hospital fare. I need to feel human again, she thought. I want to sit at a nice table and have a good dinner. Surely, they must have something like this here.

As she walked down a wide, brightly lit concourse, she noticed someone with a familiar stride and posture walking ahead of her. When she had a clearer view, she saw the woman was carrying a small child. She was sure she was not mistaken. "Ayhlean!" she called out.

The woman turned and, it was Ayhlean. When she caught up with her, Sabrina's eyes were first drawn to the child. A shock wave raced through her body. The child had Sargon's eyes.

The small boy picked up on Sabrina's reaction and made a growling sound, then told her proudly, "Me have tiger eyes."

Sabrina, shielding her emotions, took his chin in her hand and inspected his eyes. "Yes, you definitely have beautiful tiger eyes. I like them."

He smiled in response.

"What's your name?"

"Chen."

"I like your name, too." Then Sabrina looked at Ayhlean and her eyes turned a darker green. "I think we need to have a long talk."

Apprehensive, Ayhlean tightened her arms around Chen. "As long as it is just talking, I don't mind," she responded.

"Can we go somewhere, private?" Sabrina asked, mindful not to distress the child.

"Let me put Chen into the nursery. That's where I was heading. Then we can go to my apartment."

Walking to her apartment, Ayhlean was tense, sensing Sabrina's struggle to remain calm.

As soon as they were through the door, Sabrina turned on her so fiercely that Ayhlean took a step backwards. "How could you do that to me?" she said savagely, her green eyes ablaze.

Despite having expected it, the harshly spat accusation made her flinch. Gathering all her courage, she told Sabrina as calmly as she could, "Before you say anything else, I would like for you to read something."

"I don't want to read anything. I want an answer from you."

"I think this will answer all your questions," she said, going to her desk. She took out Kamila's letter and handed it to her. "This is a copy. I sent the original on to Sarah."

Sabrina gave her an irritated look, but took the letter.

Ayhlean motioned for her to sit down. "Don't stand around, make yourself comfortable. Can I get you something to drink?"

"That would be nice," Sabrina answered absentmindedly, as she began to read.

While Sabrina read the letter, Ayhlean stayed in her kitchenette to give Sabrina privacy. She did some straightening up, then, poured a fruit drink over ice. Back in the living room, she handed Sabrina the glass.

In the meantime, Sabrina had read the letter a second time, and looking up at Ayhlean, she said, "I'm speechless. Kamila wrote this? Does Sargon know?"

"Yes, some time ago."

"What did he say?"

"He wanted to know if we, in all seriousness, were going to consider it."

Ayhlean finally sat down on the sofa during Sabrina's long silence.

She openly studied her while sipping at her glass of juice. From their entry into her apartment, Ayhlean had felt Sabrina's unabated tension. Her back was still ramrod straight, and her face one big scowl. Even after reading the letter.

In an effort to ease the tension a bit, Ayhlean tried changing the subject. "How have you been? You know, I've missed you."

Sabrina, sitting on the edge of her chair, was turning the glass with both hands. "I've missed you, too," she answered automatically. "Let's get to my question first, please."

"You want to know how I managed to have Sargon's child?"

There was a very terse, "Yes."

"You remember how badly I wanted to have children? Well, let me start from the beginning. Sometime after you left, the three of us got together and had a long talk. We all agreed that we were in love with Sargon, but for reasons of his own, he'd chosen to be unreachable. Sarah and I devised a plan to get a blood sample from him to see if it was possible for him to have children with us."

Sabrina sat motionless, her face stiff with amazement. "You did what?" she asked, incredulous. "How did you manage that?"

"Wasn't easy," Ayhlean said, and laughed softly. "One day, during a sparring work out, I nick him with the foil. Sarah, very solicitous, came along to wipe off his blood. Concealed underneath the gauze was a slide. We got a good blood smear and learned he could father children with us. The next stage of the plan was to present to him how important it was to perpetuate his genes and to present it in such a way as to sound very logical. And then, not to give him a way out, even if we had to use an emotional approach, you know, like he at least owed us to have his seed perpetuated among the Antareans. Well, Kamila got to him first. She seduced him. He gave me a hell of a time. He knew all along what I was up to. So, as you can see, we broke the ice for you. He has at least agreed to let us have his children."

During Ayhlean's long explanation, Sabrina's anger slowly subsided. Her face relaxed, and some of the tension slipped out of it. Now she was simply speechless. As she digested all of it, her humor began to surface. Astounded, she finally managed to say. "Kamila, seduced him, our little Kamila?" Then, after another long pause, "Who all have children?"

"Everyone except you."

"I see."

"I have Chen, Sarah is pregnant, and Kamila has a daughter. Her name is Soraja.

"How old are they?"

Soraja is three, and Chen is almost two."

"I always seem to be the last one to catch on," Sabrina complained. "Where is Sargon now?"

Ayhlean's face broke into a broad grin. "Why? Are you going to rush off to make a baby right away?" she teased.

Sabrina's face suddenly turned bleak, and the faint shadow a depreciating smile touched her face. "No, Ayhlean, I don't think he will even look at me."

"What did you do?"

"I compromised him." And she told her the story how she left the Trefayne.

When are you going to learn not to do things like that? He must have been furious."

"He was that," Sabrina agreed.

Ayhlean looked at her watch. "I'm going on duty in ten minutes. Will I see you again?"

"No. I'm leaving as soon as I get something to eat, and after I check Spitfire."

"What's a Spitfire?" Ayhlean asked.

"A small craft that spits photons. Next time I see you, I'll tell you how I acquired it."

"The next time we see each other, I hope it will be back home. My tour is almost over. I have only one more month left."

"Lucky you," Sabrina said and hugged her. Reluctantly, she let go. Standing in the door, she said, "Take good care of Chen. I don't know when I will see you again." Then, her eyes teared. "I love you," she said softly, and quickly closed the door behind her.

* * *

Sabrina boarded her little ship after it was serviced and headed back toward the Pleiades. At her approach to the Worldship, she was hailed by Android One.

"Android One, this is Sabrina. Request permission to come

aboard."

"Permission granted."

She met no one as she rode the lift from the hangar deck to the bridge. She still believed that only androids manned the Antares. But when the doors to the lift opened, she stopped with one foot on the bridge and the other still in the lift. There was a complete crew manning the stations.

"Captain on the bridge," Chandi said in Galactic, coming to attention.

"As you were," Sabrina told them, and wondered if Chandi was pulling her leg. She had only made it to commander as far as she knew.

"Are you taking command?" Chandi asked Sabrina.

"No."

"Then get the hell off my bridge," he told her, in English. He had a hard time controlling the twitching of his mouth. He had wanted to say that to her for the longest time.

"Chandi, dear," she said dulcetly. Then in her normal voice, "I want some information that's only accessible from the bridge, so you'll have to put up with me for a minute." She went to the science station to access her personnel file. When she was unable to do so, she straightened up and turned to Chandi. Put out, she asked, "Who changed the code?"

"Sargon did."

"Well, give it to me."

Chandi went to the station, and leaning over her, put in the access code.

Her file came up. She was a captain on the Antares. It also included that she had graduated from the Space Academy of Acheron. But what was new was that she was now assigned to the Special Branch of the Space Fleet with the rank of a commander, and under the direct command of an Admiral Okada. Well, well, well, she thought, not bad. Also, she had been compensated for the time spent on the Trefayne, and for her mission with Miri. She allowed a whistle to escape, then, glanced up at Chandi.

Chandi took the bait, and reading over her shoulder, exclaimed, "How did you manage that?"

"Special talents."

"For getting into trouble?" he quipped.

She gave Chandi a quelling look and swiveled her chair around to face into the bridge. They were all young kids, most not more than eighteen years old, gawking back at her. The only one familiar, was Chandi's.

"Where did all these kids come from?" she asked, still in English.

"They're being schooled on how to maintain a worldship."

Astonished she said, "You don't say. Who's teaching?"

"I am," said a sonorous voice in English.

The speaker had been out of her line of sight, amused at their banter.

Sabrina looked past Chandi, and swallowed.

Apparently, it was male, dressed in an Antarean uniform. He had white hair, cut short. His face was dark; the nose broad, but long, with a ridge across the top. He had a wide mouth with a rather thin upper lip; the lower one was a little fuller, and with a scar just below it. Two antenna-like projections arched up his forehead like a second set of eyebrows. When she came to his eyes, she did a double take. They were slitted, but not like a cat, more like a reptile's.

Still visibly amused, he asked, "Do I pass inspection?"

Sabrina winced. Her stare must have been blatant. On a hunch she said, "You must be Karsten."

"And you must be Sabrina," he said, mimicking her tone of voice.

"I'm glad we finally met. Miri mentioned you, but didn't say much about you."

"You met Miri?"

"Yes, I did. She and I shared some fun times together, but not with Cassandra."

For a moment Karsten contemplated that cryptic remark then added one of his own. "Cassandra is a law unto herself."

Sabrina's mouth quirked. "I realized that when she threw me off her home-world."

"You didn't leave with Miri? Where's Lara?"

"They both stayed with Cassandra. I was forced to leave. Cassandra happened to have a sweet little ship she didn't need, so she let me leave in it. Then without giving me any warning, the ship went into free-fall. It was quite some time before I could access the computer."

"She gave you a ship?" Karsten asked, astonished. Then a note of disquiet stole into his voice. "Cassandra doesn't give things away. Not to strangers. Where's the ship?"

"In the hangar bay."

"Cadet Hennesee, you have the bridge. Continue with the demonstration," he told Chandi. Turning to Sabrina, "Let's go see just what it is you have been given."

Exiting the turbo lift, the ship still sat as she had parked it. A long, shrill whistle shot from Karsten's lips. "Orion," he told her.

"I was glad I knew a few words of Marathi. Otherwise, I would still be falling through space."

"Access it."

"Open Spitfire," she said, and as the door pulled back, she noted Karsten's amused look and told him, "Well, I couldn't use Open Sesame. Now tell me what we're looking for."

"We're looking for a bug, a homing device." When she gave him a questioning look, he continued, "All Orion ships have a device that allows them to find it again. Also, the Orions use their ships much like a Trojan horse. I'll bet they now know where the Antares is."

"Damn," Sabrina cursed, then, facing Karsten, "I just made it to Sigma IV. An hour before I reached the station my air ran out, and I had to use a space suit. I was in the hospital for two days. Then I visited a friend of mine. So I've had the ship for about six weeks."

"I am not blaming you. You couldn't know. Let's search the ship. Look for anything's function you can't figure out."

After two hours of combing the ship, Sabrina called, "Karsten, come look at this." She had found a device in her cot, fastened inside the hollow head-rest. "Do they like personal information?" she asked, humorously raising an eyebrow.

"Yup, you found one," he answered, ignoring her attempt at being funny.

"Now, let's see if there's one more." Going into the head, he looked into the shower and the tiny cabinet. Finding nothing there, next he looked at the toilet seat.

Sabrina, standing beside him, started to laugh. "If they put a bug in there, they heard lots of funny noises."

Karsten just looked at her, but couldn't keep a straight face. He began to laugh too. "Now I know why Miri likes you. You're two of a kind."

Soon they found one more, hidden in the hold.

"Karsten, does Sargon still have some of the resonance crystals?"

"Why?"

"I'd like to key the special effect into this ship."

Rubbing his chin, Karsten looked at her. "Wouldn't be such bad idea," he said. "You get the hook-up ready, and I'll get the crystal."

It was a long time before Karsten returned.

"Did you have to mine the crystal?" she asked him tartly.

"No, but I had some business to take care of. Let's see how much you got done," and handed her the bundle he was carrying.

He checked the tie-in to the accelerator and when he came out from under the console, "Not bad," he told her. "Hand me the cradle."

Karsten slid back under the console, while Sabrina gently unwrapped the crystal from its cocoon of raw silk. It was one of the smaller, pure, white crystals. When light fell on it, a fire swirled at its heart.

Karsten was startled when he came out from under the console. Sabrina, entranced by its inner swirling fire, and, unbeknown to her, had keyed the crystal to resonate with the energy current of her own brain-waves. His first impulse was to stop her, but on second thought, he realized it could prove to be an advantage. Karsten broke the rapport with a gentle cough.

"Enough. Sabrina, hand me the crystal."

Confused, she asked, "What did I do?"

When he explained, she only looked puzzled, not understanding.

"Never mind, when we try the special effect, we'll see if the crystal is keyed to you." While he talked to her, there was a sudden muffled growl. "What was that?"

Sabrina reddened and said, "I think that was my stomach."

"When was the last time you've eaten?

"I don't know."

Giving the cockpit a regretful look, he asked, exasperated, "Woman, do you still need someone to wipe your nose?"

"No. But I'd like someone civilized enough to take me to the cafeteria."

Wrinkling his nose at her, he said, "I think before you can go to eat, you need a shower."

"Boy, if that's not being insulted! You can come to my place and wait for me there."

"No, I couldn't do that either."

"Why not?"

He expelled his breath, puffing out both cheeks. "I think you better come with me," he said, looking pointedly at her. Her stomach had growled again.

"How embarrassing," she said, and followed him into the turbo lift.

"Deck two, level three."

Sabrina looked baffled. She had never heard of a deck two, let alone of a level three. But she chose to forgo asking questions.

When the doors opened, she let out a gasp. The doors exited onto a street. Across from it was a neatly trimmed lawn with trees, shrubs and flower-beds. A tree standing in the middle of the lawn had a familiar look. "It must be," she mumbled and walked toward it. When she ran her hand over its bole, she realized it was her tree. Her initials where there, carved halfway up its trunk.

She stared at Karsten, and her face puckered. "This is our park," she stated, holding up her hands. "But where is my apartment? Where is everything?" she asked, bewildered.

Karsten was faintly amused by Sabrina's discomfiture. "A few things have changed since you were here."

"I'd say. But, where are my things, my furniture, my books, my... ah well. What a letdown coming home," she said, incensed.

"Do you want to get something to eat, or stand here and give me a hard time?"

"I can't go anywhere looking like this," she said, sweeping her hands across her soiled coveralls. "And since everything is gone, I have no clean clothes. My duffle bag is still on the Peregrine."

"Are you always such a hell of a mess to deal with?"

"Well, if other people don't interfere and go and change everything while I'm gone. Hell, why am I standing here? I need a change of clothes. I've been washing what I have by hand."

"I expect you have no money, either," interrupted Karsten.

"Money?" she asked, her voice rising. "Since when do I need money on the Antares?"

"Since there is a bank here."

Sabrina gave him such a woebegone look that his face softened with amusement, and he relented. "I could extend you a loan until you have your business in order?"

"Where do I buy clothes?"

"Behind the hotel," Karsten said, pointing to a three-story building with a wide entrance, facing them. "Behind the hotel is a street with all kinds of shops and eateries. Let me explain some of the set-up here." Turning Sabrina around toward the building behind her, he said, "This long building is the Academy's Headquarters. Behind it, is the campus. The hotel is for visitors. Now let's go and get you some clothes. You can acquaint yourself with the rest of the changes on your own time."

The hotel lobby was nearly vacant. Sabrina and Karsten garnered some very pointed stares from the staff. Sabrina thought the only reason we are not shown off the premises is Karsten's uniform. When they exited on the other side, Sabrina just stared. There was a long tree-lined street ending in a T, and as Karsten had said, shops and eateries filled both sides with large windows and open doors.

"I'll be damned," she finally said. "Karsten, I don't need civilian clothes, just two sets of coveralls. But I do need underwear."

"Then let me take you on campus. There is a uniform shop."

"How about a shower?"

Karsten took a deep breath and slowly let it out. "My place."

An hour later Sabrina sat in a restaurant, clean and wearing a new coverall, shoveling food into her mouth.

"You know you're embarrassing? But then you always were," Karsten said.

"You talk like you've known me for some time."

"Karlana and I used to…oh damn!"

"Used to what?"

"Kept an eye on you hoydens when Sargon had to attend a meeting."

"Who's Karlana?"

"I guess I let that slip out of the bag. Karlana has been Sargon's partner on some of his missions."

"And his lover? Now, something I've felt makes sense."

There was a suspicious look on Karsten's face. "Do you read people's minds?"

"No. That's something I learned not to do. But sometimes I do get surface impressions. Especially if a person feels strongly about… whatever they're thinking."

"Sargon will not be too happy letting that slip."

With her fork halfway to her mouth, she waved her other hand negligently at him. "Aw, I bet you can handle anything he dishes out."

Before he could answer, the waiter approached their table.

"Commander Karsten, there's a call for you at the desk."

Karsten rose and told the waiter, "Put the ticket on my bill." Then he looked at Sabrina, whose eyes were drooping, and he gave her the key to his apartment. "Don't make too much of a mess," he told her and left.

* * *

After a good night's sleep, Sabrina was back working on Spitfire. When Karsten entered, he had to sidestep several times to avoid crunching computer parts underfoot.

"Woman, what in the devil's name are you doing now!" he exclaimed.

Sabrina handed him several discs. "If you don't speak Marathi, find someone who does," she told him.

"How did you get these?"

"Downloaded."

"You do not download Orion information."

"Maybe nobody else does, but I just did. And by the way, I found the real bug. The ones we found earlier were duds," she told him and handed him the device.

A whistle escaped Karsten. He turned ready to leave when Sabrina complained in a whiny voice, "Now you're leaving me with this mess, and I have to put it together all by myself."

Karsten only chuckled as he exited Spitfire.

* * *

Two days later, Sabrina had the computer back together and updated. She just decided to take Spitfire through its paces without

Karsten, when a cadet appeared at the door.

"Captain Hennesee, Sir," the cadet began. But when he saw Sabrina, he stammered, "Ma'am, I… have a m…mmessage from Commander Karsten."

"Well, Cadet, what's the message?"

"Ma'am, please. He asked that you c…come to Headquarters."

"Okay. I'll be there in a second."

"Ma'am, he m…m…meant right now. I'm supposed to escort you."

Sabrina looked closer at him and relented, hating to give the already flustered youngster a hard time. He appeared to be fourteen or fifteen. She rose, dusted her backside, and followed him immediately.

He knocked at Karsten's door.

"Come in."

When the boy opened the door too slowly for Sabrina, she pushed past him and to the cadet's amazement, exclaimed, "What's your all-fired hurry that I had to quit what I was doing?"

Karsten looked at the open-mouthed cadet. "Well, Mister?"

"Yes, Sir." He retreated hastily and shut the door.

"I don't know why I am letting you in on this, but I guess you would like to know." He motioned for her to sit down and turned on the screen. A series of star lanes, some of them shipping lanes, filled the screen, but the ones Karsten pointed to were secret outposts of the Altruscans.

"Girl," Karsten said, "the Altruscans are not going to like you. You're giving their hiding places away."

"I'll deal with it when I meet an Altruscan. Was that all I downloaded?"

"No, there's more. Something Headquarters will need to see. But I don't think I should go into it with you at this time."

"Altruscan or Orion information?"

"Sabrina!"

"Well!" Then, slipping her thumbnail between her front teeth, she frowned.

"Now what?" Karsten protested, "I don't like it when you pull that face. It always means trouble."

"Would you do me a favor?"

"I don't know. Not if it means sticking my neck out."

"Be serious. I want you to withhold this information from Doeros."

"Why, if I may ask?"

Sabrina shrugged and tilted her head to one side. "As you can guess, I don't like him. The last time I saw him, he didn't feel right. Can you bypass him for now?"

Karsten studied her for a moment. Giving her a shrewd look, he said slowly, "I could give this to Okada personally." When Sabrina simply stared, he enlightened her, "He is the Fleet Admiral. But first, I better stop at Cassandra to get more information about your ship. Then we'll stop at Daugave and have a talk with Okada. Would you care to come with me?"

"What a dumb question."

Chapter 12

Spitfire sat untied in the hangar-deck. It took most of an hour to get the Aurora Borealis serviced and Karsten packed, ready to go. The Aurora Borealis, like Miri's ship, was made of the same dull gray material, but in flight, if light shone on her, her surrounding energy fields lit up like an Aurora Borealis.

Karsten's ship was also much larger and more luxurious then the Peregrine. It had a lounge with a bar and dining area. Also, the kitchen was more spacious than the little cubicle on the Peregrine. There were three bedrooms with a toilet and a shower. Maintaining all that luxury was a being, a...Sabrina didn't have a name for it. When she asked Karsten, he called it a Shela. The Shela was neither human nor animal. Karsten said it was something in-between, a genetically created, non-gendered life form. It was sentient and could speak English.

"Mad scientist?" Sabrina asked, raising her eyebrow.

"Did Miri tell you about him?"

"Just enough to wet my curiosity."

"I see. If you need something, just ask Shela," he told her.

Later, when she met Karsten's first mate, she did a double-take, then, gave Karsten a questioning look.

"This is Teva," he told her. When she looked at Karsten and then at Teva, Karsten chuckled, "This time it wasn't the mad scientist."

"I'm Sabrina, nice meeting you."

Teva only nodded.

Teva reminded her of Lara. The same tawny eyes, red mane, and blue tint to his skin.

"Come to the bridge, and make yourself useful." Karsten told Sabrina.

It didn't take her long to realize that the Aurora also had the special effect keyed into her computer.

After they cleared the Antares, and were reaching warp speed, Karsten activated the special effect. A bell chimed and Sabrina shut her eyes tightly as she felt the power-surge of the engines. Then there was a sense of nothingness, not of hearing, nor of feeling. When the bell chimed twice, the ship decelerated and Sabrina opened her eyes. Cassandra's world stretched before them, filling the screen.

Karsten established orbit.

"How long will you take?" Sabrina asked.

"Just long enough to get answers. Why?"

"Cassandra doesn't like me."

"Okay. I'll be back soon."

Karsten returned with a very somber expression on his face. He was very short with Sabrina, avoiding her questions as he took the pilot's seat. Clearing Cassandra's World, he again activated the special effect. When the ship decelerated, Daugave rotated beneath them.

Karsten docked the ship at the space station, orbiting above the planet. The station looked very much like a giant pinwheel. Finished with settling the Aurora Borealis, he and Sabrina beamed down to the planet and materialized inside the transporter room of the headquarters building.

"Let's get something to eat first. We have two hours before seeing Okada. And please, will you stop running around in coveralls," Karsten pleaded.

"I'm an engineer. Engineers wear coveralls."

"I give up. I simply give up on you."

"Good, then let's go and eat," Sabrina replied.

Exactly two hours later, Karsten and Sabrina presented themselves to the adjutant in the outer room of Okada's office.

"Commander Karsten, reporting."

"Commander, go right in. The Admiral is expecting you."

"Thank you, Lieutenant."

Sabrina stared when she saw Admiral Okada. Okada was squat and compact, oriental in looks. His unlined face seemed ageless. His silvery hair made a striking contrast to his black eyebrows and his bright, black eyes. He looks like an older Yoshi, Sabrina thought.

"Admiral Okada, may I introduce Commander Hennesee?"

Okada gave her an icy stare. "Ah, so, this is Doeros' nemesis." As they were still at attention, he said irritably, "Sit down, I hate to glare up at people." As soon as they were seated, he leaned toward Sabrina and asked, "Why did you want Karsten to by-pass Doeros?"

Sabrina swallowed. "Sir," she said, then cleared her throat. "There is no apparent reason I can give you. Lately, being in his presence leaves me with a curious feeling of something not being quite right; like there is something I'm missing."

While she spoke, Okada looked through a folder. The admiral grunted as he sent her a skeptical glance. "She has ESP?" he asked Karsten.

"Captain Thalon has tested her; she has a high score."

"Says here that he believes in her hunches."

Sabrina half rose from her seat, "I'll...say..."

"You will say nothing young lady. Sit back down."

Sabrina fell back into her seat. She lowered her head, but managed to continue looking at Okada.

"Also, you will refrain from rifling my files," Okada told her sternly.

"My, Sargon...Captain Thalon must have sat here and babbled a lot about me," she said indignantly.

Okada ignored her and turned to Karsten. "I have withheld this from Doeros. I want you and Commander Hennesee to go on reconnaissance and then report your findings back to me," and he handed Karsten a disk.

The disk Okada gave Karsten was information about two planets called M, 3 and M,6 in which the Federation was very interested in.

Chapter 13

After the Altruscans had been persuaded to stop using Coronis as a weapons-testing ground and the arachnids for target practice, they discovered a small star with one planet and two moons and deemed it suitable for their purpose. They named it M, 3. The planet was a dry world with very little water; the atmosphere was thin, but livable. The terrain varied with mountains and deserts.

When Karsten and Sabrina approached M, 3 the space around the planet appeared to be free of patrolling ships, but, Borealis' sensors picked up a large troop encampment in the vicinity of the desert. They waited until the middle of the night before landing in a small shuttle on top of a low hill. The shuttle was made of the same material as Miri's Peregrine. With its dark, non- reflective hull, it was nearly invisible. Also, the material deflected sensors.

After disembarking, they climbed down the hill until they found a small hollow and set up camp. Their reconnaissance could wait until morning. Then wait again till nightfall, using night-vision goggles to invade the compound.

When morning dawned, Sabrina and Karsten stared in dismay at a storm brewing on the horizon, and at the growing cloud of dust.

"Not a very auspicious beginning," Karsten said.

"We could go down Orion's shield-arm and inspect the next solar system," Sabrina suggested.

"Might as well. What do you think about calling in Miri?"

84

"That wouldn't be such a bad idea. We might need her special talent," Sabrina agreed.

The shuttle lifted during the height of the dust storm when any sensor -sweep from the ground would be blocked. They soon docked on the Aurora Borealis. Once outside the small solar system, Karsten contacted the Peregrine and gave Miri the closest intersect point. As the Borealis dropped into real space, Miri was already there, waiting for them. After docking the Peregrine on the Borealis, she walked briskly onto the bridge demanding, "What took you so long?"

In lieu of an answer, Karsten put the star chart on screen and waited for Miri's comment.

"From your little ship's computer?" she asked Sabrina.

"It yielded some of the Orion's not so well-known trade routes, and as far as we could decipher, the information of two planets we think the Altruscans are using for military purposes. We tried to investigate M, 3 here," Sabrina said pointing to it, "but we were prevented by a sandstorm."

Miri studied the star-chart, then turned to Sabrina," Since you're sitting at the navigation console, why don't you lay in the heading for M, 6 and then, how about doing galley duty? While we eat, we could decide who will be first to have the bridge."

"I only volunteered once to be your kitchen slave," Sabrina reminded Miri.

Miri turned back from the chart and looking with unfocused eyes at Sabrina, then smiled. "True, but you were such a huge success."

"Okay. Only this once," Sabrina answered, emphasizing each word with a jab of her finger. "Now, what about Shela?"

"She keeps the ship neat, but doesn't know much about cooking," Karsten told her,

When the door closed behind Sabrina, Miri turned to Karsten. "Why did Sabrina ask to bypass Doeros?"

"She told Okada he didn't feel right. Do you know anything more about it?"

"I almost agree with her. Lately, there's something not quite right about him. What else was on the discs Sabrina downloaded, besides the trade routes and the two planets?"

"Some very interesting correlation of names; individuals high in the Alliance's hierarchy, and I think the Orions have grown suspicious of the Altruscans."

"Not bad for us. Maybe we should prod them a little by releasing some interesting information."

"After we're through here, I think I'll talk to my Orion friend."

* * *

It was during Karsten's shift that the Borealis approached the second solar system and the planet marked as M, 6 on the chart. After turning command over to Teva, he helped Miri in the galley, then, rousted Sabrina out of bed. He conferred with them over a hot meal about what strategy to employ.

"We could park, waltz in, and tell them to show us their facility," Karsten remarked to Miri.

"And end up corpses before we take a second step?"

Sabrina suggested a more cautious approach and proposed they reconnoiter the three moons first. The three orbs proved to be unlivable and the landscapes barren, even forbidding. Lastly, they orbited the world below.

Miri was in the process of taking sensor readings. "How do you like winter?" she asked Sabrina.

"Only, if I'm at a ski resort with a tall mountain and a lot of snow."

"I don't think there's much of a civilization below. The only energy reading I get is at the northern polar region. And it's weak."

Rubbing his chin, Karsten had been hovering over Miri's shoulder. After he called Teva to the bridge, he told Miri, "Why don't you take the Borealis out of orbit and farther out into space after Sabrina and I beam down? You remember the asteroid we've seen tumbling close to the second moon? Position the ship behind it."

When Teva appeared, and after briefing him, Karsten told him to take the bridge.

After Karsten and Sabrina were dressed in warm clothing and had filled their backpacks with the necessary equipment, they beamed down close to where Miri had picked up the energy readings. Karsten's life-scan registered a small outfit. There were only a few people on that icy world.

"Sabrina, what do you make of this?" he asked after making another sweep, then holding the scanner under her nose. "I've never seen anything quite like it. It registers as energy, or maybe some kind of life-form."

"Let's find out what's inside that electrified fence."

Before them was a flat expanse and several buildings surrounded by a fence. As they approached, suddenly there was an incongruous sound, barking.

Sabrina looked at Karsten. "Dogs?" she whispered.

Karsten only shrugged, and motioned for her to retreat.

As they made their way around a small ridge, it began to snow. It was a wet and kind of clinging snow, whipped by a wind, its velocity steadily increasing. Disgusted, Karsten said, "I think we're jinxed. First, the dust storm, and now I guess we'll have a snowstorm. What do you suggest we do?"

"We could get to the lee side and find shelter. At least until Miri is overhead with the Borealis."

But Miri did not come back, and as they waited, the falling snow grew heavier. Sabrina began to shiver. Pulling Karsten's hooded head toward her, she yelled into his ear, "I think we better find some shelter."

Karsten only shook his head. "No, girl," he yelled back. "There won't be enough time for that. What we need is to build one. Ever make an igloo?"

"No, but if it gets us out of this cold and snow, I'm game."

Instead of building an igloo they tunneled as deep as possible into a snow bank.

* * *

When Karsten awoke next morning, it was even colder. Lifting his head from under the cover, his breath froze the instant it left his mouth. He was about to lay back down when he realized the little dugout was all lit up. As he looked up he saw Miri squatting in front of him with two steaming cups in her hands and she had brought a lantern with her.

Miri looked amused. "I thought we were on a spy mission and I find you in a love-nest all cuddled up," she said, her lips pursed.

Sabrina and Karsten were lying close together inside one of the water-proof sleeping bags, sharing the warmth of their bodies, while the second sleeping bag was draped over the top. Karsten looked down at Sabrina and then at Miri. "Did you know she snuggles?" he asked Miri.

Sabrina lay curled up and as close to his body as possible.

"It's cold. What do you expect me to do?" Sabrina complained, as she pushed up on one elbow and reached for the cup. "Where have you been? Sleeping all nice and warm on the Borealis?"

"I haven't slept. I was chased by a surveillance probe and had to pretend I was a comet. I had a deuce of a time getting rid of it. I hope what showed up on their sensors was a rock with its tail streaking by."

"I bet we rung the doorbell," Karsten said plaintively as he climbed out of the sleeping bag. "How's the weather, Miri?"

"Hellish."

"That's what I figured," he said, listening to the wind howling outside. "How are we going to find out what they are doing here? I don't think this weather will let up." Turning to Miri, "Would you mind popping over to see what they have behind that electric fence?"

When Miri left, Karsten and Sabrina wrapped themselves in their sleeping bags and sipped the hot drink. Later, Sabrina became antsy with the inactivity, but more so by a growing feeling of foreboding. She went outside to investigate. The storm-driven sleet felt like needles hitting her face. Visibility is nil, she thought, and quickly ducked back inside.

"A good thing Miri came along. We would have had to scrub this last part too," she told Karsten, drying her face on one of his dry mittens. "I don't think this storm will let up."

Karsten only looked at her with a worried expression on his face. It seemed that a vast stretch of time had passed since Miri left. According to his calculation, she was taking far too long.

When she finally popped in, her shoulders were all hunched up, and alarmed, Karsten picked up the lantern and shone the light into her face. Miri looked gray, and there was horror in her eyes. Pulling her into his arms, "Report, Miri," he commanded, but spoke it softly.

Miri looked startled, like someone who'd just awakened from a nightmare. Her face was drawn and her large hazel eyes were glazed as she looked up at Karsten. Then she crumbled against him.

"Miri, tell me what happened," he anxiously asked, and lifted her face.

She only stared up at him with sunken eyes.

Sabrina, alarmed, tried to touch her, but Karsten, alerted by her movement toward Miri, reached out to prevent it. But he was too late. Miri was wide open. Sabrina could feel her mind screaming from unimaginable horrors. What Sabrina read in Miri's mind were memories from the time she and Karsten had been held captive. For Sabrina it was a de-ja-vu of Elisheba's withdrawal. But for Elisheba it had been her body, for Miri it was the rape of her mind. Sabrina, horrified by the emotions, turned ashen as every trace of blood drained from her face. Tears began to flow as she reached out to enfold Miri and Karsten, allowing her compassion and love to flow between them.

They remained for a long time in each others embrace.

Disengaging gradually, Sabrina asked softly, "Miri, did Thalon teach you how to clear your mind?"

Miri shivered in response, then, shook herself. Taking a deep breath and expelling it in a long, audible sigh, she finally said, "Yes, he did."

"Why don't you use it now? Reach deep inside to that center-core. Touch it. Let go of the feeling of hate and despair. It is only tearing you apart. Let the light in; let it dispel the darkness."

Sabrina pulled Miri back into her arms and their minds joined. Sabrina began lending Miri her strength when she faltered on her journey inward. Karsten's mind followed, he was awed. He had touched something in Miri, something bright and undamaged by the horror. He was first to come out of the trance and softly touched Sabrina and then Miri. "We still have a mission here," he said, calling them both back into the real world.

Miri shuddered and then her hand went to Sabrina's face, touching it gently. "No wonder Thalon loves you," she whispered. Then she pulled herself together and said, "Let me get the Borealis first, then I'll beam you up. We are finished here."

On board the ship, Miri pretended to be back to her normal self and busily sat at the console. She activated the screen first, then, next, inserted the recording she had made.

"What the devil!" Sabrina exclaimed.

On view was a small room with four people sitting naked on stools, forming a circle. Two were adults; one was a young girl, the other a small boy. When the viewer zoomed in on their faces, horrified, Sabrina realized that their eyes had been gouged out. "Those people have been blinded," she whispered. Suddenly there was a movement from all four corners and ovate energy patterns in red or pink colors converged on the people. The small boy's frightened voice rang out, asking, "Is anybody there?" He received no answer. Instead the energy patterns elongated and each enfolded one of the victims. After that, the ovate forms turned opaque. Sabrina could tell that Miri's hands had been shaking as she held the recorder to wait for further developments. One of the ovoids, the one enveloping the small boy, divided. There were two energy patterns where before there had only been one. The one which had enveloped the girl was next to divide. The two who had encased the adults divided into four sections, becoming four ovoids. Miri's recorder pointed to the thermometer, showing falling temperatures. When the temperature reached below freezing, the ovoids became lethargic, and their color turned to a dull gray.

"Oh God, that's monstrous," Sabrina exclaimed, physically shaken. Even experiencing it only vicariously through watching the screen, she was affected by its raw horror.

"Yes, after that, I just had to get out of there."

"Was there anything in particular you noticed?"

"Yes Karsten. Something you and I have smelled before, a sweet, sickening scent. You know the one in those vials. The ones we opened and the liquid simply evaporated."

"And it came from those ovate creatures?"

"Yes."

"I wonder what they are."

"Maybe Thalon knows something."

"You want Thalon to see this first, before we show it to Okada?"

"Yes Karsten. He might remember something we don't."

"All right, let's go with that. Miri you look exhausted. Why don't you turn in? Sabrina and I will mind the store."

"Thanks Karsten, I think I will."

After Miri left, Karsten looked at Sabrina, "Back to M, 3?" he asked.

"Might as well." As he turned to the navigation console, Sabrina noted that his face was still drawn and ashen.

* * *

The first time they approached M, 3, it had looked like a quiet world. Now, warships involved in mock battle were surrounding it.

"How are we going to get down there?" Sabrina asked.

"Just as before, at dusk. For now, we will stay back and monitor their communications."

It soon became apparent that the Altruscans were practicing invasion tactics, training their troops for a planet-wide invasion. Shortly before nightfall, they heard the command for the ships to stand down. Miri, still shaken by what she had discovered, was ordered by Karsten to remain on board and out of sensor reach.

The flyer descended rapidly through the atmosphere. Sabrina leaned forward to watch the view-screen while Karsten's sensors scanned for life-readings. Again, they landed in the little hollow and after orienting themselves, immediately made their way toward the compound. Although the base was no more than two miles away, it took over an hour to cross the dark and rough terrain. They had taken an indirect route. When they reached the first building, Sabrina rested against the wall, and asked, "Any life readings, Karsten?"

"There seem to be only two or three people inside."

The building was a cube, perfect on every side. They ducked under several windows before reaching the door. It was unlocked. By sheer luck, the first building they entered was the headquarters. Inside, in the eerie glow of the red night light, the corridor seemed deserted. All was quiet. As they crept along a passage, Karsten shone his flashlight at the doors, reading the name plates. The fifth door down was the commandant's office. His Name was Garth bar Za-or. Karsten grunted when he read the name. Sabrina looked at him questioningly, but he only shrugged his shoulders at her.

After opening the door, Karsten whispered, "Get any information you can. I'm going to find the communication center and then, I will join you."

Sabrina nodded and stepped inside. She quickly went though Commandant Garth's desk. It was immaculate with few papers on top, they were of no importance. But, there was a map on the wall Sabrina paid close attention to. The computer, an outdated model, gave Sabrina little trouble to rifle through. With her eidetic memory, she memorized the most important points, and just finished shutting down the computer when the door opened and a guard stepped in.

"Shht. Put that gun down," she told him in Marathi. "I saw movement in here, so I came in to check."

A scowl flickered across his face. "Who are you?"

"I'm Lepar. I just came in with Stormcloud. I'm assigned to Commander Votar," she said, pointing toward a door farther up the hallway. A good thing they had monitored the ship's communications. She remembered a female named Lepar being ordered down to the planet to assist a commander Votar.

"First, you do not look Orion or Altruscan. And second it doesn't explain what you are doing here."

Sabrina smiled briefly and shrugged her shoulder. "I left a computer disc on commander Votar's desk and was on my way to retrieve it when I thought I saw light in here."

He took a communicator from his belt and called Stormcloud.

"Lieutenant Moro here. I have a female called Lepar. She says she is from your ship, assigned to Commander Votar?"

"Correct. She is a computer technician. She left this morning to go planet side."

"There, Lieutenant Moro, I check out," Sabrina said and started to walk away when a tall, reedy figure came toward them.

The guard came to attention. "Commandant Garth," he said.

"Who is this?" Garth asked.

"This is Lepar. She is from Stormcloud."

"Sir, I am a computer technician assigned to Commander Votar. I saw a light move in your office. I went to investigate, but there was no one in there."

"Someone activated my computer," Garth stated.

"Sir, I didn't touch your computer. It is a somewhat seasoned model I haven't seen one like this in a long time."

Garth reached out and slapped her across the face. "Woman, you only speak when spoken to. I did not ask you a question."

Sabrina's hand went to her cheek and she lowered her eyes. Then she did something she should have done before. She mind-touched tenuously at first, just enough to determine whether he had ESP. When she was certain he did not, she riffled his files. She quickly learned that he had an inflated ego; that he was cruel and could turn nasty. Probing deeper, she found his mind busy with an invasion plan. It was a small solar system similar to Earth's. With the map already imprinted on her photographic memory, she now knew its position. As she began to read his short-term memory, she was appalled by it. She had infuriated him by calmly answering his questions without the awe he thought his due from females. His mind was already undressing her, and she sensed his arousal.

"Search to see if she has anything hidden on her body," he told Moro.

When Moro looked at him in confusion, Garth took a knife from his belt and sliced the front of her coverall open. "Turn around," he told her.

As Sabrina turned, she felt him slice down the back of her coverall. When she came around to face him again, his mind was already busy with the imagined pleasure he would have bedding here.

"Check her boots."

Moro bend down and pulled her boots off. "There is nothing," he said.

"All right, you can go now. I will take care of this."

Sabrina studied Moro as he rushed off, sensing his distaste and fear. When her eyes moved up to Garth's face, there was a slow grin growing, spreading his thin lips as he looked at her body. Her shredded coverall lay crumpled on the floor.

"Come," he said imperiously. When Sabrina tried to kick at him, she nearly stumbled over her torn clothes. She kicked them out of the way and backed away. He struck her, brutally, with his open hand; then, followed with a punch to her face. "Bitch, you will come when I tell you," he said, and suddenly grabbed her, throwing her on top of his desk.

Oh no, you don't, Sabrina thought. What surprised her was the unexpected strength of his thin body. She was about to fling herself at him when she felt a momentary mind-touch and remained still. Garth had just loosened his belt and was zipping down his pants when the transporter beam took her.

When she materialized on the shuttle's transporter platform, Karsten at first stared speechlessly at her. Naturally, she was in her birthday suit, and his face changed through a host of fleeting emotions. "Not very elegant, Sabrina," he finally chocked out.

"Aw, shut up Karsten, and help me up."

"You're going to have a beaut of a shiner," he told her, as his fingers gingerly touched her face. "By the way, Miri put your duffle-bag in your cabin."

"Good. That son of a b…"

Before she could finish, Karsten coughed and put up an admonitory finger. "Ladies don't use such words. What will the world come to when nice girls use dirty language?"

"Karsten!" she said, exasperated. Then she began to laugh. "Well, at least I have some clothes to change into."

Much later, and back on the Borealis, she entered the bridge, and Miri asked, "Why aren't you asleep?"

"Where are we going?" she answered with a question.

"Back to Daugave. Now, how about you go to sleep."

While Sabrina was asleep, Thalon came aboard the Borealis and looked at the recording Miri had made of M,6, and Karsten gave him everything he had down loaded at M, 3.

* * *

Sabrina stood watch on the Borealis as they orbited Daugave when a message came in for her. She was to report to Admiral Okada, immediately. She turned the bridge over to Teva and beamed down to the Headquarters building. As she entered Okada's office, Karsten and Miri were rising to leave.

"Where are you two going?" she asked.

"Commander Hennesee! You will observe military courtesy." Okada ordered.

"Yes Sir," Sabrina said and saluted smartly, then turned around and asked again, "Well, where in the world are you going?" Sabrina's ear caught the creaking of a chair and sheepishly explained, "Sorry, Sir, but if they run off, I don't have a way to get back home."

Okada suddenly chuckled. "Thalon warned me about this young

woman, but I just wouldn't believe him," he said to Karsten. Turning to Sabrina, "I want you to sit down and be quiet," he ordered and waved for Karsten and Miri to leave.

Once the door was closed, he studied Sabrina with an unreadable expression. Finally he said, "Commander Hennesee, in one hour you will take command of the Corvus. Here are your orders. I advise you to familiarize yourself with them. Dismissed!"

Sabrina rose, saluted, and left his office with a mass of conflicting thoughts racing through her mind. She looked at her orders and then at the closed door.

"Damn, damn, damn! I want to go home," she muttered. "Now, where could Karsten and Miri have gone?" On a hunch she went to the officer's mess and walked up to their table. "You two, tell me, how I've ended up in this muddle?" she asked tartly, pointing to her orders.

Miri affected great patience when she answered, "Sit down Sabrina and we'll fill you in." When Sabrina had settled into her chair, Miri continued, "We handed the report and the map you drew to Okada. He has ordered the Corvus to intercept the Altruscan ship, but the Captain of the Corvus had a medical emergency, so, you are ordered to take over. You had your big tantrum on the Trefayne, now you have to pay the consequences."

Sabrina gave a big heaving sigh. "Miri, if you weren't my friend… you are my friend, aren't you?" she asked with such a woebegone expression that Miri's stern face relaxed, and she chuckled.

"Miri, would you get me something to eat while I study this. I only have an hour." Then she looked across at Karsten, "Do you have any advice?"

"The Corvus has never had a female crew member, let alone a captain. They are from Madras, and somewhat chauvinistic," Karsten informed her.

Sabrina only groaned.

Chapter 14

The doors of the turbo lift opened and Sabrina stepped onto the bridge. All heads turned.

The first officer, Commander Dahl, began, "Cap…" then, stopped.

All eyes were focused on her and she felt a brick wall go up. It was just as tangible. She could almost hear their thoughts.

"As you were, and it's Commander," she told them, and stepped up to the command center without hesitation. The center was elevated so its occupant could observe the crew working on the bridge. She took the captain's seat.

Around the room, it was dead quiet.

Sabrina leaned back in the swivel chair and, with a glint in her eyes, surveyed the bridge. "Status report?" she asked.

"Sir, Ma'am…"

"Sir, will do," Sabrina told the first officer.

The first officer quickly checked over all the consoles. "Yes, Sir," he said, abruptly. "All moorings are cleared, Commander. The station reports we are ready to depart. Bay doors should be opening."

The Corvus rotated slowly and hovered until the doors of the space-dock opened.

"On screen." Sabrina watched the doors retracting, and after they were open, ordered, "Thrusters ahead one quarter."

The impulse engines took the Corvus beyond the space dock.

"Navigation, bring up chart."

"Heading?" the navigator asked.

Sabrina studied it for a moment. "Thirty-six, mark five. How long to initiate warp?"

The ship shuddered, and then hovered.

Sabrina quickly looked up and gave the consoles a quick scan. Then she hit com. "Engineering!" When the engineer answered, she asked, "What's wrong?"

"Chief Engineer, here. We seem to have a problem," he answered.

"What kind of a problem?"

"I am working on it, Ma'am."

Gossip traveled fast. The crew already knew they had a female captain.

"Commander Dahl, you have the con."

Sabrina sped to the turbo lift. When she arrived at engineering, she paused in the open doorway. Her first impression was that it was clean and well run. She looked at the men standing around, most with a smug expression on their faces.

She read them well. They had no intention of being commanded by a female. Everyone on the ship knew that the Captain was to be released from the hospital within eight hours. So engineering had decided to use a little delaying tactic. She found the Chief Engineer in the office off the main section. Sabrina glowered at him, and he returned the look. This could develop into a battle of wits, she thought. She raised her chin and looked at him with weary eyes, then asked, "How far is the power down?"

"Power is reduced at least by half."

"I see." Sabrina went to the console and brought up data on the current status of the engines. She studied them for a while, then left his office and returned to the main engine room and went to the energy flux regulator.

"I think we have a small obstruction here," she told the Chief Engineer, who had followed her. Taking the needed tool from a nearby crewman, she removed the blockage and expertly calibrated for normal flow. "This will be the last problem we'll be running into," she told the Chief in a calm and reasonable voice. Looking around, she added, "The place looks clean; well run."

The Chief's mouth had hung open in surprise and consternation. It closed and then opened long enough to respond, "Yes, Ma'am,"

She went to the intercom. "Bridge!"

"Bridge."

"Commander Dahl, accelerate to full impulse power."

Her last glimpse of the Chief Engineer was of a man biting his fingernails and then awarding her a speculative glance. On the way to the bridge she smiled. No engineer would damage his engines, so it could only have been a small problem, easily fixed. Before stepping onto the bridge, she made sure the smile was off her face. It would be bad policy to give the impression of being easy going.

Back on the bridge, she opened inter-ship communications. "This is Commander Hennesee. I am in temporary command of the Corvus. Our orders are to intercept an Altruscan ship heading for Omicron V. Since the situation could prove dangerous, I'm counting on your full cooperation. To simplify things, I'm addressed as, Sir."

The Corvus headed out of the Pleiades toward the Orion's arm at warp six.

On the bridge, Sabrina turned to the navigator. "Lt. Raga, transfer trajectory onto the main screen and plot intercept point." Turning to the science station, "Commander Dahl, compute speed and time to reach intercept point."

"Aye, Sir." Dahl raised his head, "We will arrive at intercept point just short of seven hours from now."

"Good. That will be time enough to have a drill for battle readiness. I want to gauge how well the crew performs," and to herself she thought, and it won't give anyone time for more mischief.

"Inform the crew I do not want one hundred percent. I expect one hundred and ten percent efficiency. Commence drill."

* * *

Sabrina had just come out of the shower when her communicator beeped. "Hennesee," she answered.

"Commander Hennesee, we're tracking a vessel, but the configuration shows it to be an Orion ship, not Altruscan."

"Noted. I'm on my way."

When she arrived almost immediately on the bridge, the officers looked at her in surprise. She had been prompt. The grid showed the ship's position on the main screen, displaying its trajectory and the intercept point.

"We're still on target to intercept within the hour," Dahl told her.

"Good. Go to yellow alert."

Forty-five minutes later red alert sounded throughout the ship. Battle readiness was established almost instantaneous. Sabrina watched the tactical display. It showed a long range scan of its course, their approach, and the intercept point.

She felt a tightening of her stomach when the Orion ship materialized starboard of the Corvus.

"Ready, Mr. Maden?" Sabrina asked.

"Ready and in range, Commander. Commander Hennesee, we surprised him. Their shields are not even up yet."

"Mr. Maden, target the Orion. Fire photon over his bow."

"Firing, Commander!" The Corvus gave an internal shudder as the torpedo launched. Sabrina held her breath. The Orion's shields went up almost instantly, as they dropped into real space with the Corvus right behind. Slowly, the Orion rotated toward them.

"Mister Maden, arm every weapon we have. Be deliberate about it. Let them see and scan." She waited another minute or so, then, turned to the communications officer, "Hail them."

"Incoming message, Commander."

"Put it on screen."

The screen shimmered, then, displayed the bridge of the Orion ship. She nearly let out a sound in her surprise and had to suppress a grin. The Orion's face was perfectly round, with nearly translucent white skin, and no hair. He beamed at her with a bonhomous smile which turned instantly into a look of surprise. "A beautiful lady?" he fluted with a mellifluous voice. "Ah, if it were not for the distance, I would be at your feet."

Sabrina controlled her amusement and let only a thin smile crease her stern face. "Ah, what chivalrous words from the mouth of a pirate. I'm sorry to have to turn this badinage onto a more serious track. I must ask you to refrain from your intentions for the world beneath the lovely sun of Omicron V."

"But Madame," he said, his voice taking on a plaintive note, "All the players are in place, and it would be a shame to interrupt such a well-orchestrated production. Besides, how do you intend to stop us?"

For some time, Sabrina had felt a delicate mind-touch alerting her that Karsten was in the vicinity. "By calling in the cavalry," she told him. She thought-sent, "Now!" and promptly the Trefayne and the Explorer dropped out of warp-space. "Sorry, but I insist," Sabrina said to the now scowling face of the Orion.

The Orion saw that he was outnumbered and slowly rotated his ship, moving from mach to light speed, then into warp.

"Commander, incoming message from the Explorer."

Karsten was on screen. "Commander Hennesee, the captain of the Corvus will be beaming over, and your next assignment is to command the Trefayne."

"Thank you, Commander Karsten. May I have permission to retrieve my duffle bag first?"

Since Sabrina never fully unpacked, it took her only a short time to arrive at the transporter room.

The captain of the Corvus, having beamed over from the Explorer, was curious to meet the female who survived his crew.

"I hope you didn't have too difficult a time," he said, his face crinkling at the laugh-lines around his eyes and mouth.

"Oh no, nothing less than manageable," she told him with a bright smile. "Captain, you have command."

"I have command. Thank you, Commander Hennesee."

Sabrina saluted, then, stepped up to the platform with a whimsical look on her face. "They're not Chirons," she told him.

* * *

The Trefayne was on scientific assignment when Sabrina took command. Once she was on board she was informed that Captain Estel was on six month leave. Also, Chief Engineer Ian McPherson was not on board either. Sabrina pursed her lips, but when she saw the transporter engineer's curious look, she immediately slammed her mind-shield down.

When she stepped off the turbo lift, Commander Dan was on the bridge.

"Welcome on board, Commander Hennesee. You have the

bridge."

"Thank you Commander Dan. I have the bridge."

"Our mission this time is the training of several young scientists. The destination is the molecular cloud in the vicinity of the Trapezium."

"You're telling me we have kids on board?"

"No Commander, young scientists."

That was as close as a Chiron will ever come to being humorous, Sabrina thought as her eyes fastened on the distant stars. "Then it should prove an interesting journey," she said.

She moved over to the helmsman to study the controls for a moment, then the main screen, which was on maximum magnification. Nothing showed out there then the ever-present stellar background and the immense void between the stars.

* * *

If the Chirons thought Sabrina to be a token captain, they were mistaken. She took an active part in the daily routine of directing meetings and the ordering of the bridge, even taking part in some of the classes. She took pleasure in being around the young people.

Bending over the head of a twelve-year-old Chiron, she watched him trying to plot the absolute visual stellar magnitudes along a vertical axis.

"What are you planning to be? Maybe an astronomer, or a physicist, or an astro-physicist?" she asked him.

He cocked his head to look up at her. "My father is an astrophysicist and I'm expected to follow in his footsteps. Were you expected to emulate your parents?"

"No. My father was a physicist and my mother a biochemist. I'm an engineer and I also teach science, and right now, I'm a commander having to act like a captain."

He responded with a quick glint in his eyes, then, told her, "This is my first astronomy class and I'm trying to recall the classification of stellar magnitudes."

"It's easy when you remember that the higher the magnitude, the fainter the star; the lower the magnitude, the brighter the star."

"Thank you, Commander," he mumbled.

She ran her finger along a diagram, "This is called the main sequence. It is running from the upper left corner containing the hot, massive blue and blue-white stars, down the middle where the lower temperature yellow and orange stars are. At the bottom right corner are the cool, small red dwarfs."

Dan had just entered the classroom and walked up to her. "Commander?"

"Yes, Commander Dan?"

"You are not required to tutor our youngest scholars."

"I am aware of that, but I enjoy teaching."

Dan gave her a nod, but his eyes moved toward the professor whose frown was very discernible.

"I see," she said, then mumbled as closely as she could get in Chiron, "Spoil sport." Dan compressed his lips, but the boy suddenly ducked his head and sneezed to mask a giggle.

Estel had warned Dan not to underestimate Sabrina, or to expect her to behave like a Chiron. Dan knew this to be an understatement and suspected his captain to have been humorous. The last time Sabrina was on the Trefayne she walked off the ship, catching everyone off guard. Dan had never met anyone like her. Estel told him that he once asked Captain Thalon to explain Sabrina, but Thalon only pointed to Ian McPherson saying, if anyone can explain her, he could. Ian naturally denied it with I never try to explain females, Sir.

Sabrina left the classroom, heading down to Engineering. Chief Engineer Ethan indicated that his department was running well and under control. Last time she had been attached to his department as an insignificant ensign. But he deigned to talk to her for a while, and also gave her several engineering data disks to catch up on new innovations.

* * *

Slowly everything settled into a routine. Sabrina had little contact with anyone, except the bridge crew. By taking command, she freed Commander Dan to work with the budding scientists, shuttling them back and forth to various positions in the Trapezium. Her life before boarding the Trefayne had been hectic; there had been little time even for a breathing spell. Generally, she preferred it that way. And as before, the Chirons were courteous, but did not avail themselves of her company. She had to find things to keep herself occupied.

There were too many empty hours when she was off duty. Now she had to deal with the horror of M, 6. Through her link with Miri she had gained an insight into the atrocities of that experience, and now it became part of her emotional memory.

Coming off-duty late one evening and not really tired, Sabrina decided to look for books she had on tape. She sat on the floor and rummaged through her duffle bag. The first tape that came into her hand was one from her interstellar law classes. She had been carrying them around since leaving Acheron, and she looked at them with mixed feelings. Acheron, she thought and shuddered. She had no intention of ever going back. Acheron could be likened to a spider's web which trapped her into personal involvements for which she had not been prepared. She shivered and with loathing thought of Machir Aram. Suddenly her anger flared. He's probably bragging about it, or thought he got away with it. She balled her fists, pressing them against the sides of her head and shuddered. She was having flashbacks, and was experiencing the rape and the humiliation. Again, she saw the smirk on his face as he removed her clothes while she lay drugged and helpless on the bed. Worse than the pain from his battering, was the knowledge that she had only been a thing he used to enhance his ego.

She sat stiffly upright on the floor, her fists raised, tears were stinging her eyes. The intensity of her rage surprised her as the memories came flooding in. She remembered all of it, again felt the humiliation, the shame, and the helplessness. Suddenly she realized she was broadcasting her thoughts and emotions, and immediately slammed down her barriers.

Later that night she awoke with a start from a nightmare with her heart pounding and her hair was wet. The ovoids! Oh God! In her nightmare everything had been tangled up with Machir Aram's face, the ovoids, and a gigantic spider web, and being trapped in it!

Of a sudden a faint glow appeared in her room and to Sabrina's utter amazement a cowled figure walked slowly toward her bed. "Sabrina, Child," his voice said softly.

"Huh?" The only thing visible in his face was a faint smile and then a whimsical down turn of the mouth.

"You are broadcasting your emotions throughout the ship."

"Good God, I thought I was awake," she mumbled, rubbing her fingers through her short hair. "Are you real, or a ghost?"

"I'm real."

"Who are you?"

"My name is Sabot."

"How did you get in here? How did you get on this ship?"

He only showed her an enigmatic smile.

"What are you doing here?"

"There will come a time when we will work together. I know you remember the ovoid energy patterns."

"Yes, and…What do you know about them?"

"They are the reason I am here. But for now I came to help you. Strong emotions, even if held tight, break through at unexpected times. You have not been dealing with some of the terrible experiences you had," he chided. "As long as you hold them in, they will haunt you. Think Child! Who is hurt by your anger? Whom are you hurting with your hatred? Why do you keep your feelings so tightly locked inside? Think clearly, Child, you hurt no one but yourself. Bring those painful memories forward and look at them. While I shield you, let them go; use the techniques you have been taught."

Sabrina's vision turned inward and a whole range of emotions scurried to the surface while her mind struggled to focus on the truth. He was right. She was the only one being hurt by her own hatred and anger. Fear could impair her ability to function and think clearly where the ovoids were concerned.

When she looked up, the cowled figure had vanished and her room was again in darkness. What on Sam's Hill, she thought, I must still be dreaming. What was it? An apparition? She had to concede that no matter who or what it had been, the advice was good. She could not afford to broadcast her emotions or leak out at unguarded moments, especially not on a Chiron ship. Sitting up, she let herself drift slowly into a meditative state. One by one she brought the memories forward and examined each of them, letting herself feel the rage and horror. Using Sargon's technique of changing energy with energy, she built up a roiling black cloud and filled it with all her hatred, the animosity, and the horror. Visualizing a wind racing through the churning cloud, she let it all scatter as if it were a time-lapse video. She went through the process several times. During the last time, as she watched the cloud swirling by, she visualized the sun breaking through. She let herself feel the warmth and joy and freedom at its breakthrough. She went back to sleep, imagining that she was lying with her bare skin on a sun-warmed beach.

Next morning when she stepped onto the bridge, there were some curious looks from the crew. I really must have broadcasted my nightmare, she thought. She still wondered if the monk had been an apparition or not?

Chapter 15

"What will you do when the Trefayne goes to Khitan?" Commander Dan asked her several weeks later.

"If there is a way, I would like to get back to the Antares while the Trefayne is being refitted. I know it would be out of the way. But could you manage it?"

"Yes. I have already asked for permission to make the detour," Dan said as he watched Sabrina's rising eyebrow.

"You have anticipated me," she said.

"We will pick you up in two months."

When the Trefayne approached the Antares, they were hailed by Android One.

"Android One, this is Sabrina. Have me beamed aboard."

Back on the Antares she went to the bridge. "Android One, who is on board?" she asked.

Sargon is on board. Shall I notify him?"

"No."

She decided to get herself a hotel room before getting in touch with Sargon.

After a shower, and then a meal in the hotel's dining room, Sabrina decided to check whether Ayhlean was already on board. She was about to call the bridge from the hotel's office, when to her surprise, she saw Joran through a window walking across the plaza. On a hunch, she followed him. She was right behind him when he entered the headquarters building and headed toward a turbo lift. She entered the lift just as the doors were closing.

"Hello, Joran," she said pleasantly. "How long have you been on the Antares?"

"Sabrina!" His whole face lit up. "When did you get back?" he asked surprised, and immediately pulled her into his arms.

She let herself be hugged, and he kissed her passionately before she could say, "Just now."

"Are you back to stay?"

"For a while. How are you doing? Are you here with Sargon?"

"Yes. He thought I should have an idea about the world you came from."

"Oh. So he did."

The lift stopped at a level unfamiliar to Sabrina. Joran stepped off and crossed to a door. Sabrina sensed Sargon behind it. "Joran, let me talk to him privately. He will call you when he has need of you."

"Will I see you later?"

"Yes, I will see you later."

Joran had no idea that no one knew where Sargon's quarters were, and Sabrina was not about to enlighten him. She slowly opened the door and slipped into the dimly lit room.

"Joran, did you get the report down to Ayhlean?" Sargon asked. He had obviously just come from taking a shower. There were still beads of water on his shoulders and only a towel draped around his waist.

"I guess he did," Sabrina answered him.

Sargon spun around. "How did you get in here?"

"Through the door," she told him, pointing over her shoulder.

"Where did you come from?"

"The Trefayne.

"I guess I need not ask you who let you in."

"Nope."

"What do you want?"

"To have a talk with you."

"Can't that wait until later?"

"No. I think this is just about the most perfect timing," she said, looking at his towel with a pointed expression. "What I came to see you about is…when I was on Sigma IV, guess who I ran into? There was this wee little laddie who told me he had tiger-eyes."

Sargon chuckled. "I see you met Chen." The corners of his mouth twitched to hide his smile. Here we go again, he thought with the same amusement he felt with the other girls. He wondered what tactics Sabrina would use to approach that subject.

"Yup, that's what he said his name was."

"So?" Sargon asked, while shrugging his shoulders.

There was a long "Sooo," from Sabrina while she walked slowly toward him, and quickly snatched off the towel. "I think you know all about the cute little idea Kamila had. I'm claiming house-rights."

"I don't think so."

"Oh yes I am." She tried to push him, but he stood unmovable as a rock. "Damn, can't you just for once, cooperate?"

"I see no reason to."

"I see, what you're trying to do is prolong this game."

He stood half-turned toward her as she stepped as close as possible. Experimentally, she ran her hand along his arm, and he didn't move away. Slowly, her hand continued across his chest. She pressed herself against him, her face leaning on his shoulder. Her whole body was now in contact with his. When her hand wandered down beyond his abdomen, she found his response to her. Her response was a sharp intake of breath. Suddenly, she bit him savagely on his shoulder, drawing blood, and then liked it off with her tongue.

Sargon's breath came in a deep grunt. He turned fully toward her and teased, "I see you like to play games, too," and slowly began to unzip her coveralls. They dropped unheeded to the floor as he reached to undo her bra.

"You seem to be experienced," she mumbled into his ear.

"I'm a quick learner."

Sabrina only giggled. Shyly, she reached up and cupped his face with both hands and kissed him. All the emotions and longing for him were in that single, long kiss. For a time she was content just to stand still, to feel her body touching his.

Sargon patiently waited. When his arms embraced her, he let her feel his passion. Their minds joined and she was shocked by his powerful sexuality. Like a bud unfolding she opened to him and joined in the play of his mind, in the arousal, and then in the mingling of their needs. She soon felt herself lifted as Sargon carried her into the next room.

* * *

Sabrina remained with him all that day and night. Next morning, when he left, she called Ayhlean and asked if they could meet at the hotel.

Ayhlean, entering the lobby, immediately caught sight of Sabrina. She stood by the reception desk, looking somehow preoccupied and forlorn. After they hugged, Ayhlean's first question was, "When did you get back?"

"Two days ago."

"Then you saw Sargon?"

"Yes," she said wearily.

"Boy, you're short in the answer department," Ayhlean griped.

"Sorry, Ayhlean. I've seen Sargon, but he has shut me out again."

Ayhlean smiled, and asked, "Did you try Kamila's idea?"

Sabrina only looked at her, then, said, "Yes. He made it clear he went along with our scheme to avoid being labeled a party-pooper. Then he told me that he considered to have complied with our house-rights, and nearly threw me out of his quarters.

Ayhlean gave her a sympathetic look. "But at least you will have his baby."

Taking a deep breath, she gave Ayhlean a frustrated look, and lowering her voice, explained patiently, "Ayhlean, I don't want his baby. The way my life is, I have no time for an infant. The only thing I ever wanted was him. Now I am where I have always been."

When Ayhlean saw Sabrina fighting tears, she gently touched her on the arm. "Let's go to my place." Silently they walked across the busy plaza when Sabrina abruptly stopped. "I still can't get used to all the changes and all the people," she complained.

Ayhlean gave her a sympathetic look. "I know. The good old days are gone. Working on the space station made the transition somewhat easier for me. But I still miss our park. You know the tree you carved your initials in? It's still standing."

"Yes. I found the tree and was shocked when I realized that I was looking at what used to be our home." Then she smiled ruefully, thinking of Sargon's note she had kept all this time, telling her of her childhoods ending.

Ayhlean pointed to a lift. "Here's where we go to the cells."

The lift first traveled sideways and then up, and when the doors opened, Sabrina thought she would at least recognize the nursery cell area. But when she exited the lift, she stepped into a park. "Where's the hallway?" she asked in astonishment. "And where is my place?"

Ayhlean laughed at her discomfited look. "We are in the top layer of the nursery cells. Yours is a level below."

When Ayhlean opened the door to her place, Sabrina exclaimed. "Oh Ayhlean, this is beautiful," as she stepped through the portal onto a graveled path. Both sides of the path were lined with flowering shrubs. As the path wound on and around a curve, they came upon a vaulted bridge spanning a tiny brook. After crossing the bridge, to their right was a small lake, its blue water disturbed by the paddling of several swans. On the left, out of a dell, rose a three-storied, eight-sided pagoda, crowned with the distinguishing, upward-curving roofs.

When Sabrina stopped to gape, Ayhlean chuckled. "I took some architectural liberties with traditions. This pagoda is built to live in." When they passed the front entrance, Ayhlean gestured to it, explaining, "The entrance hall is large and I plan to have it tiled, but haven't decided what motif to choose. Come, let's go around back to the kitchen and have some tea." Ayhlean's kitchen was very modern, but decorated in the country style Sabrina found familiar.

Before they sat down at the table, Sabrina waved her off with, "Give me some paper while you brew the tea."

When Ayhlean came to the table with the steaming teapot and cups, Sabrina handed her the paper. "You think that would do for a motif?"

Ayhlean looked at the drawing and laughed. "I can't understand why I never thought of it. Of course, a Chinese dragon."

"The dragon needs to be in red, and the rest of the tile should be in contrasting colors."

"Do you have a motif for your house yet?"

"I don't know, Ayhlean. I can't put my mind to anything, except that in less than two months the Trefayne is returning to pick me up."

"And you don't want to go?"

"No. My life has been so topsy turvy and so much has happened. I need for things to slow down so I can get a handle on it."

Suddenly the door burst open, and a little boy propelled himself into the kitchen followed by Sargon.

"Hi Mommy, I'm back," Chen crowed at the top of his voice and crawled into Ayhlean's lap. "Daddy says he got to go to work again," he informed her.

When Ayhlean looked questioningly up at Sargon, he said, "I have a mission and should be back in two months, maybe." When Sargon glanced at Sabrina, her face puckered. She was close to crying and turned her head away. "Sabrina?" he asked gently. But she only shook her head and began to weep. For a moment, he stood still. He thought to go to her, but bit his lip instead. He turned and swiftly walked out.

When the door closed behind him, Ayhlean set Chen down and slid from her chair. Kneeling beside Sabrina, she put her arms around her waist. Sabrina's face was white, a blinding misery clouding her eyes. Her head came to rest at Ayhlean's shoulder and she sobbed.

Ayhlean uttered comforting, meaningless sounds, stroking Sabrina's hair. But Chen was not at ease with this scene and pulled on his mother's hand. "She must not cry," he commanded. "Big girls don't cry."

Ayhlean started to laugh.

Sabrina brushed her tears away and reached out to gently touch his head. She told him, "Chen, sometimes little boys and big girls have to cry when they hurt. Could you give me a big hug to make me feel better?" she asked.

Chen held out his arms for Sabrina to pick him up. She held him close for a while, taking comfort from his tight embrace. But it was not for long. Soon he wriggled and demanded to be set down. With a deep sigh she watched him running and making growly noises in his throat, pretending to be a tiger.

"At least Sargon cares for him," Sabrina said to Ayhlean.

"Oh, when Sargon is here, he collects him and Soraja as often as he can. Did you know Kamila is back? He probably had both at his place. Chen says that he has a big place."

"Then, it's not the apartment near the bridge?"

"No. Those are his quarters. From what I can glean from Chen's prattling, he has another place…Come to think of it I never asked you if you had somewhere to stay."

"No. But I rented a hotel room."

"You could stay here."

"Thanks, Ayhlean, but I don't think that would work out. Do you still have the list I gave you way back when?"

"What are you going to do?"

"I'm going to build my villa. So that next time I come back, I have a home to go to."

"Most of the material you wanted is stored in your nursery cell."

"Can I get some robots?"

"Tomorrow soon enough?"

Chapter 16

Sabrina was now spending most of her time working on her villa. Today, she decided to quit early and get something to eat. Breakfast had been some time ago, and her stomach had begun to growl, which she found annoying. When she arrived at the cafeteria, it was full. She scanned the crowd and surmised that most of the students were not Antareans. As she made her way through the line, she saw Sargon leaving with Karsten and several dignitaries, and wondered what was going on.

For some time she had been curious how the bit and pieces she had uncovered were related. And she wanted to know if there were any new discoveries about M,6. The memory of the ovoid energy patterns still preyed on her mind.

With tray in hand, Sabrina walked up to Chandi who was absorbed in grading test papers he had spread across his table. He had yet to notice her. Unfortunately, there was no extra space, so she moved to an adjacent table. He did not notice her until she bumped his table.

"Sabrina, I don't have time to visit," he said with a distracted expression,

"Chandi, I am still second in command, even when I'm not on the command roster," she reminded him.

"Okay, okay big sister, what is it?"

"What's with all the brass?"

"It's an inspection tour of the Antares. They're being shown everything except the family quarters. Those are off-limits."

"So, they're only seeing what Sargon wants them to see?"

"Naturally. Now what's the real reason you're hassling me?"

"Sargon's itinerary."

"Why?"

"Like I said, I'm still part of the Antares even if I appear to be on loan to everyone else."

"Want to come back home?"

"Yes. Now my question, please."

"Why don't you eat before everything gets cold?" Chandi reminded her.

"Okay. I'll eat, you talk."

While she shoveled the food into her mouth, Chandi filled her in. "The brass should be leaving about now, and Sargon will be on the bridge in another thirty minutes."

"What about the strange kids here?"

"While you were gone, Sargon opened an Academy to train cadets. They're going through the same curriculum we went through. The kids are aged fourteen years on up. He also opened a bank and a trading center. And...the Antares is now a stopover for ships traveling between the Pleiades and Hyades. The stopover is on the other side of the ship, and as far as I know nothing connects the two sides."

"Where is Yoshi?"

"He is on Daugave and Benjie is on Acheron assigned to the Space Academy there. Kara is teaching here and Meghan is, I don't know... somewhere. I haven't seen any of them for some time."

"And you?"

"I'm working with the kids here, mostly under Commander Karsten. I'm his flunky."

Humph," Sabrina said with a full mouth. After she swallowed, "Chandi, how busy is he?"

"You mean Sargon?"

"Yes."

"He's off duty."

She cleaned the last bit off her plate and was about to rise.

"Sabrina, even if I'm not second in command, I would like to be kept keyed in as well."

"I want a briefing from Sargon, especially about a few things I discovered."

"And you ain't telling me?"

"Nope. You probably should get back to correcting whatever you have here."

"You know, you're as exasperating as Sargon."

Sabrina only gave him an amused look, then, drank the last of her protein mix.

Chandi leaned back in his seat and looked at her with exaggerated disgusted. "Big sister, better wipe your mouth before Sargon sees you."

"Oh, do I have a mustache?" She cleaned her mouth on the napkin, then with a wave of her hand walked briskly to an intercom on the wall near the entrance. "Bridge."

"Bridge, here."

"This is Captain Hennesee, is Captain Thalon on the bridge?"

"Yes. Just a moment."

"Thalon. What do you want?"

"Meet me in the briefing room," she said and hung up before he could respond. In her minds eye, she could see the scowl on his face. But she knew he would come. She had to wait a while, but didn't mind, since it gave her time to compose herself. When the door opened, Sargon stepped in with Karsten in tow.

"Well, hello gorgeous," Karsten greeted her with a suspiciously, bright smile.

"Sargon interrupted, "Okay, I'm here."

"Chaperon?" Sabrina asked, pointing to Karsten.

There was a momentary quirk to Sargon's smile as he sat down and folded his arms across his chest.

"I want a briefing on all the changes made on the Antares and the reasons. Then I want to know about all the undercover stuff," Sabrina demanded.

Sargon shot her an amused look, but Karsten had to comment, "She doesn't want much, does she."

"She never does," was Sargon's reply. "Primarily, we are a member of the Planetary Alliance, which comes with obligations. The credit is due to Serenity and the contrivances of a few others. Very few people knew how sparsely the Antares was populated..."

"Okada knew?"

"Yes, he and I are old friends. Also, to operate a world ship, one needs resources..."

"That's why the mining operations?"

"Yes, Sabrina. And if you continue to interrupt me, we shall be here all day."

"Oh, I don't mind. Feels like the good old days."

"You miss them?"

Sabrina gave him a mournful look. "Did it ever occur to you that I could be homesick?"

"Yes, it did, but to answer your questions, there was the mining of minerals and ores which were sold to space stations. The money was used to finance you kids' education. Also, to maintain the ship, funds have to flow in. The academy was expanded to include students from other worlds. The trade center was also set up to generate revenues. Then to manage all of it, we needed a banking system..."

"And what about the other side?"

"Same reason. The Antares will change as she grows. Where it will lead, I don't know. It will be interesting to watch."

"Well, when you go away, you'd like your home to remain as you left it," Sabrina said. "Now, how about all the clandestine affairs? Since I was somewhat involved in them, I'd like an overall picture. I want to know as much as *you* know," she remarked, stressing the you.

Sargon gave her a thoughtful look, followed by a glance at Karsten.

It was Karsten who continued the briefing. "We have been following the Altruscans' activities since we became active in the Orion sector. It's a long history and maybe someday I'll tell you. But for now, let's see. As you know the Orion hegemony allied themselves with the Altruscan confederacy, and for a long time we thought the Orions were the bad guys. Foremost, the Orions are merchants. They trade, buy and sell anything people are interested in, even other human beings."

"Including vice?" Sabrina asked.

"That too. The Altruscans on the other hand are military. They have a military dictatorship. Since wars are costly and deplete a nation's resources quicker than anything, there is a constant need to expand to other worlds to get raw materials. Usually, when they take over a world, the first thing they do is kill off the leadership. Then the conquered people are enslaved to work in the mines and factories. In addition, they round up the young people and put them into military training camps. Once they are trained, they're immediately shipped off to other planets, or ships. The tapes you garnered from the planet with the little boy you so rudely dropped in, showed many of the Altruscans' old alliances. They were using that planet as an agricultural base. Most of the people were herded into collective farms to produce food for the Altruscans. As the soil became depleted and the venture unprofitable, the planet was abandoned, and with it the Altruscans who ran it. The tapes from Spitfire, showed some of the Orions' trade routes, but we already knew them. They also revealed Altruscan outposts which were new to us. The Orions naturally spy on the Altruscans."

Earth is still on the Altruscans' itinerary, so we will keep an eye on that. M, 3 is a desert world, uninhabited. M, 6, the one you worry about, is undergoing an ice age and is unpopulated as well. What the ovoid energy patterns are, we don't know. Neither do the Orions. When we apprised them of the facts, they became highly alarmed. By the way, the Captain of the Orion ship is a friend of mine, and he is interested in making your acquaintance."

Sabrina blinked. "You do have interesting friends, Karsten," she said, eyeing him with a gleam in her eyes. "You know when I was a kid I always wanted to meet a pirate. Do they all have bald heads?"

"They don't have a single solitary hair on their whole body."

"You don't say," Sabrina said, wide eyed. "Not anywhere?"

"No. Not even..."

Sargon quickly interrupted, knowing that if he let Sabrina and Karsten continue, the two would soon try to outdo each other bandying jokes around. "We still don't know what the ovoid energy patterns are, or where they came from. The Orion Captain hinted that the Altruscans were getting too secretive and might be planning a coup. They've become suspicious of the Altruscans, even frightened."

Sabrina sat looking past Sargon, her expression a pensive one, her thumb nail jammed between her front teeth.

"You know," Karsten said, looking at Sargon "when she looks like that..."

"She's laying an egg..."

"Aw, cut the cackle," Sabrina told them both.

When the laughter died down, Sabrina said, "In all seriousness, the ovoids bother me. The Altruscans do nothing without a reason. I bet those energy patterns are dangerous to handle. Why put themselves at risk, unless they are planning some atrocity? This has haunted me ever since I saw Miri's tape."

"We'll keep on top of it," Sargon told her reassuringly.

Karsten then asked, "Do you recall Miri saying that the odor from the ovoids smelled familiar?"

Sabrina nodded.

"Lara is going to find out more about them."

"How?"

"I think Miri mentioned the mad scientist…"

"Frankenstein."

"Very apropos. His assistant …"

"Igor," Sabrina couldn't help commenting.

"As you wish," Karsten said, then, chuckled. "He helped us once and we thought to locate him and asked him about the ovoids. He may know what they are or where they came from."

"Will you keep me informed?" she asked Karsten.

"Yes, of course."

She turned to Sargon. "And the brass today?"

"Show and tell."

* * *

Sabrina straddled a pipe when Joran walked into her nursery cell. "Exercise or work?" he asked, carefully choosing his way across the partially finished floor.

"I guess you could call it both." She wondered why he had come. Her conscience still troubled her where he was concerned. She had promised to see him after she came on board. Instead, she had stayed with Sargon. Because of the emotional turmoil and her bad conscience, she had avoided him. Reluctantly she asked, "What can I do for you?"

"I don't know if you can do anything for me," he said, trying to keep his feelings out of his voice. But then the disappointment crept in. "I waited, but you never came."

"I'm sorry, Joran. What do you want me to say?"

He drew in his breath to speak. "Say you care about me."

"Joran, you know I do," she said quickly.

"But there's a big 'but' there. I left the house of Sandor to be with you. Did you know that?"

"Joran, no! That was a foolish thing to do."

For the first time he looked directly at her; his face touched with self-mockery. "I know. Then, when it comes to you I am a fool. I'm still hoping that you cared for me."

Sabrina turned a rueful face to him. "I do care, Joran," she said gently. "But I can't be your wife. I can't marry you. Don't ask me why."

"But I am asking ... and I do know. His voice slightly altered in pitch, just a fraction higher, as his throat tightened. "You're in love with Sargon, aren't you? You stayed with him."

Sabrina compressed her lips, angry with herself. "You want a confession? Yes, I'm in love with Sargon. I have been ever since I was seventeen." Then she laughed, a low sound, utterly without pleasure. "Don't worry, he doesn't want me. He threw me out when I asked to stay,"...or did beg to stay? She looked at Joran. "You know we're in the same boat. At least, I haven't thrown you out."

"Couldn't you just accept me?" Joran asked, quietly.

Sabrina winced and bit her lip. She was at a loss. Still straddling the pipes, she looked at him without speaking for several moments, then, decided to use her PSI awareness. At first she couldn't find words. She even felt embarrassed by the intensity of his emotions. But, finally, she understood him and what he was asking of her. The least he wanted from her was to be part of her family. He wanted to have her name. It was a matter of pride for him to be able to show that she had accepted him.

"Joran, you put too much emphasis on belonging. We don't belong to anybody but ourselves..." Sabrina halted; then, she said more slowly, "No one owns anyone. I guess it was slowly in dawning. I always felt because of all we went through together, and the way I feel about him, that Sargon belonged to me. He had become so much a part of me. But he belongs to himself. This is what he was always trying to tell me. Oh Joran, I've been such a fool. Talking to you now has brought it to the surface." She slowly rose and grunted, her hand massaging the pain in her lower back.

"Where are you going?" Joran asked, confused.

"To the registrar's office to put your name on my family-tree. Isn't that what you want?"

"Yes," Joran said slowly and then sighed.

"I know. But that's all I can offer you, my honesty about my feelings for you, and my friendship." When she turned to the door, it opened and to her surprise Sargon walked in carrying Chen. "I need a favor," he said without a preamble.

"I can guess. You want me to babysit."

"Yes, could you?"

"Sure. Joran and I were just going to the registrar, and then to get something to eat." When Sargon's eyebrows rose, she quickly added, "Don't get your hopes up. You're not off the hook yet. I'm just entering him as belonging to my house."

Sargon gave her one of his long looks, then, handed Chen to her. Affecting a teasing attitude, he told Sabrina, "I didn't know how much trouble you were going to be when I promised your mother I'd take care of you."

"Chen, what are we supposed to say to that?" she asked the little boy.

Finally able to get her attention, Chen voiced the most important thing on his mind. He put both hands to her cheeks," Sabrina, we're going to go eat ice-cream?" he asked, looking hopefully into her face.

"Did you promise him that I would get him some ice cream?" Sabrina asked Sargon.

"Well, I had to bribe him, otherwise he wouldn't come," he told her, biting back a grin.

"Does Ayhlean know where he is?"

"Yes. I left her a note to say that you volunteered to babysit."

"Humph," Sabrina said. "Being captain doesn't give you the right to play tyrant. Come, Joran, let's go before he thinks of something else."

At the registrar, she was surprised to see an unfamiliar girl seated at the computer. She was told that Ayhlean had left to attend a meeting.

"Are you taking her place for the duration?" Sabrina asked.

"I'm Commander Thalon's secretary," she replied in a no uncertain tone.

"Okay, Miss Secretary, would you be so kind as to bring up my file on your computer. My name is Sabrina Mary Hennesee."

The girl complied and Sabrina scanned her records. "There are some alterations I will have to make," she said to Joran, and to the girl, "Would you mind moving over and let me at the keyboard?"

"Only authorized personnel are allowed to handle files," the secretary informed her.

Astonished, she looked at Joran. "Now we have a bureaucracy on the Antares, too. First there was a banking system I had to deal with, and now this."

"I established the banking system," Joran told her. "It was the reason Sargon brought me to the Antares."

"Well, that's a letdown. I thought I was the sole reason you came here," Sabrina teased him.

Confused, the secretary looked at them. "Now, would you please tell me what I can do for you? Except, handling the computer."

"Well, let's see," Sabrina said slowly, looking with a designing expression at Chen. Then she put the boy down on the floor. Chen, finally able to move freely, went to explore this new environment. He bent over into an open drawer, and soon papers were flying out onto the floor.

"Oh my goodness, he's making a mess," Sabrina said facetiously, while watching the exasperated girl. Since Sabrina made no move to restrain the child, the secretary picked him up and sat him on the floor. Then she started to collect the papers he had strewn all over.

With the secretary thus occupied, Sabrina seated herself in front of the computer and next to her name Sabrina Mary Hennesee, she put ra Thalon, and then added Joran's name as Joran Sandor ra Hennesee. She turned to Joran, "Now, you're legit," then leaned back to watch Chen's antics.

He's quite a handful, she thought amused. Every time the secretary thought she had things under control, he found something else to get into.

Finally, Sabrina relented and picked Chen up. "Well, I guess you can't help me," Sabrina told the girl.

Ayhlean's secretary eyed her with suspicion. "What did you do to your file?"

"I amended it."

"But you can't do that."

"Oh yes, I can. I'm Captain Sabrina Hennesee. Thank you for your assistance."

The secretary, back at the computer, brought up another file. "You're not on the command roster. You're not even listed on my civilian file. You have no standing here. I have to call …" The door opened, and she let out an audible sigh of relief. Chen, with a big whoop, scampered into his mother's arms.

"Hi Joran," Ayhlean said. Then she gave Sabrina a sharp look. "Are you giving my secretary a hard time?"

"Oh no, I would never do a thing like that. But I did make an unauthorized use of the computer," she told Ayhlean before the secretary could say anything.

"What did you do?" Ayhlean asked, suspiciously.

"Commander," Sabrina responded, putting Ayhlean in her place. Then, mischievously added, "It's about house-rights. I added 'ra Thalon' to my name. That should help make it legal. We can legislate on it when everyone is home again. I think I heard you say hi to Joran. Do you know each other?"

"We sit in on some of the same meetings," Ayhlean explained while she opened Sabrina's file again. "I see." When she looked inquisitively at Joran, Sabrina quickly injected, "as a family member."

"Oh, I thought you finally did the proper thing."

Chen felt he had been forbearing long enough and pulled his mother face around so she would have to look at him. "Mommy, Sabrina and I are going to eat ice-cream."

"Are you spoiling this child?" Ayhlean wanted to know.

"Me? Never! Sargon's bribe, so he would come with me." Sabrina took Chen from Ayhlean, "A promise is a promise, right Chen?" Then to Ayhlean, "Pick him up at my place."

Chapter 17

Sabrina received the message that the Trefayne was on its way to pick her up just as the robot hoisted the last column in place. I guess the second story to my villa will have to wait until I get back, she thought ruefully and massaged her lower back, which had been bothering her since she had started the work. You're out of shape, she told herself. Maybe I just need a good workout. She hadn't been to the gym for some time.

The drains were in place, all the pipes had been laid and hooked up, and the electricity worked. Her first floor was finished, and the shell for the fountain in the courtyard had been poured. The two months had seen a lot of progress. Her Roman villa was taking shape. Feeling very content she stepped back and accidentally bumped against a portable light. She reached out to straighten it when her eyes followed the light beam toward the cell wall. The wall flickered, lighting translucently from within. Inside the wall, dancing reflections of colors became visible. She could see all the primary colors and a multitude of shades, and probably some her eyes couldn't register. They were swirling, rising and falling as they intermingled, then separated. Bewitched, Sabrina moved closer to watch. She became mesmerized and found herself unable to break the hypnotic spell. An intense feeling of disquiet crept over her. It took an effort to finally break free from the entrapment.

Abruptly she turned away and shuddered, then quickly turned off the light. Her immediate action was to contact Sargon. When he answered, she asked, "Have you ever noticed the hypnotic effect the nursery cell walls give off?" she asked him.

"Yes. But it only happens if an intense light shines at them."

"What do you think the purpose of it is?"

"Purpose?" he asked, surprised.

"Yes. There has to be a reason."

"A hunch?" he asked.

"I don't know. It's a feeling I was left with after the swirling colors pulled me in. It scared me when I couldn't break free. There isn't a message in it, is there?"

"I will consider your observation and investigate. I heard the Trefayne is on her way. I wish you an interesting journey," he said, signing off before she could reply.

"Oh you're a genius in rubbing me the wrong way," she grumbled.

She picked up the list of requisitions she had been working on this morning, then, went in search of Ayhlean. As she walked into the office, Sabrina face looked like a thundercloud.

"Let me guess," Ayhlean said, "Sargon?"

Sabrina stared at her for a moment, not comprehending, then laughed out loud, "What else is new?"

"Is that another list for me?" Ayhlean reached for the requisition sheet Sabrina held toward her.

"I don't know when I will be back, so just stow it in the cell like last time. Another thing, have you ever seen the swirling colors within the walls of the nursery cells?"

"No. What are you talking about?"

I happened to shine a bright light on it and colors started swirling around inside the wall. It was hypnotic. I have a hunch, and it's only a hunch, but since they are nursery cells that could only mean offsprings, something to do with the early inhabitants' young, perhaps. What I'm getting at is, don't let Chen look at the walls when they are illuminated. I told Sargon about it and he said he would investigate further."

"Are you serious?"

"Like I said, it's only a hunch."

"Okay. I'll keep it in mind. Would you like to have supper with me tonight?"

"I wish I could, but the Trefayne is on her way. I'm saying goodbye.

Until I see you again, take care." She hugged Ayhlean, holding tightly onto her for a moment, then said, "Give Chen a kiss from me, will you."

After the door closed behind her, Sabrina leaned against the wall and let out a deep sigh. She wished she could stay home.

* * *

The moment the Trefayne was in range, she beamed over.

"Captain on the bridge," rang out, as she came out of the turbo lift.

"As you were," she told the crew. "Commander Dan, what's our assignment and where to this time?"

"Captain Hennesee…" he stopped when Sabrina turned abruptly to face him, an eyebrow questioningly raised." You have been promoted, Sir."

Sabrina's acceptance was an expelled breath and a "humph" thinking how in the hell did I manage that?

"The Trefayne is on her second return trip to Khitan to resupply. We were called to exchange crew members on a patrol cruiser. Our arrival time at Khitan will be in seventy-two hours. We are picking up a group of scientists and a team of archeologists. Our next destination is a dying planet on the outer fringes of the Hyades. Here is the memorandum outlining our assignment," Commander Dan said, and handed her an envelope.

"Thank you, Commander." Sabrina turned to Lt. Rodan, "Lieutenant, sensors forward and ahead, warp two."

Sabrina watched the screen for a moment knowing that behind her, the Antares was falling away. She felt a twinge of regret. Seated at the con she activated the ship's log. She listened to it over the ear phone while she read the orders Dan had just handed her.

The archeologists quest was a dying planet where a survey team found several ruins that might be remnants of a larger city. The finding was deemed significant enough to warrant an exploration. And, the leading scientists were interested to learn why life on the planet became extinct.

* * *

Sabrina was sound asleep when her intercom chimed. Instantly awake, she activated only the voice circuit. "We have reached destination," Commander Dan informed her. It took only a short time to brush her teeth, slap water on her face and slip into her uniform. A short run-through with the comb and she was ready. When Sabrina entered the bridge, a reddish tinged planet filled the viewing screen. Aware of the Chiron's efficiency, nevertheless, Sabrina asked Commander Dan if he had initiated sensor sweeps.

"I have, and there are no detectable life forms, water sources, or plant growth," he informed her.

The corner of her mouth moved up a fraction, "Have you readied the shuttle yet?"

His deep voice held a hint of amusement. "No. I deferred to wait for your orders."

She liked this gentle Chiron. Although usually taciturn, he had never given her a feeling of aloofness, like most of the Chirons during her short stay on board as an ensign. She cast a quick glance at Lieutenant Tamar, remembering the incident and smiled. Considering their long life-span, Tamar was still young for a Chiron.

* * *

Some time before dawn, the shuttle touched down at the edge of a red, sandy desert. In the forefront were hills, appearing mauve in the gray dusk. Behind them, jagged mountains pierced the sky like stone spires. Overhead the cloudless sky was a strange silvery grey, and the pale ghostly white sun just coming over the horizon gave off little warmth. Only a few ruins were visible above ground, but aerial photos had shown traces of buried structures reaching far out into the desert.

As soon as everything was unloaded, the camp-site quickly became organized into a tent city. Within three days, it was operational and the archeological team settled down to the serious work before them. By then the scientists had left camp with their equipment. The archeologists used the aerial photos to mark off their sites. Soon they began digging trial trenches and test pits, using probes made of metal rods driven deep into the ground. Each rod was tipped with a hollow metal ball that trapped earth to be brought to the surface for analysis. By the end of four weeks, the archaeologists had found six different layers of civilization. Now began the arduous task of stripping away these layers one by one.

Sabrina observed everything with absorbed fascination.

* * *

Late one afternoon, Sabrina diagnosed her current edginess as cabin fever; the ship was closing in on her. She decided to beam down and maybe help the archaeologists with their work. She enjoyed digging and scraping away at the foundations being unearthed. Although her back still bothered her, she hoped working would make her forget her queasy stomach. Usually, just moving around in the fresh air helped.

When she materialized at the site, she was glad for the cloak she had brought along, and wrapped it close around her. Already the meager warmth of the desert day was giving way to a bitter dry cold.

Several days ago, the archeologist found a second city, and Sabrina was eager to see it. Part of it was built into the steep walls of a canyon and had not been visible from the air.

As she moved cautiously down into the canyon, she found a winding staircase cut into the fantastically eroded walls. Soon she came upon palaces and temples carved into the living rock. The stone-cut structures were of imposing scale. Some of them were three to four stories high.

She entered one of the temples. It was awe-inspiring; the vaulted ceiling was reminiscent of cathedrals. Underfoot was a marble floor and still standing were mottled marble pillars with elegantly carved capitals supporting the roof. When she entered the palaces, she found painted murals of geometric designs. But nowhere could she find pictures of people or even animals. Inside, in many of the palaces the columns and roofs had fallen and she had to scramble over pillars and debris.

Outside again, she came upon a bend and saw the city itself. She was amazed how well everything was preserved. It had been built where the sandstone cliff curved inwardly to form a shallow plain, sheltering the city from the desert winds.

Sabrina watched for a time as the archaeologists worked away under the glaring arched lights, digging more trenches and trial pits. After a while she wandered out into the desert. She needed solitude. She was worried. Of late she had been losing weight, and frequently felt nauseated. Even thinking about eating had become a problem. Sitting down on a rock, she let herself relax, gazing out over the barren landscape where distances seemed to lose their vagueness. Ranges of chaotic and broken hills, scores of miles away, looked but a moment's walk.

Surprisingly, a sand storm appeared on the horizon. The cloud swelled with amazing speed, churning toward her. She barely reached the mouth of the canyon. When she turned around, coming out of the cloud of sand were tank-like vehicles shooting photons, and overhead, airplanes roared past, spitting fire.

Sabrina panicked and ran for safety behind a stone parapet. As she watched, she noticed there were no impacts from the photons or from the fire overhead. Then, as suddenly as the phenomena appeared, it collapsed within itself. Not sure if what she had seen was real or an imagining, Sabrina called up to the Trefayne.

Commander Somar answered.

"Somar, did you track a very short-lived phenomenon just now?"

"Yes, it showed on our sensors. Curiously, it was localized, and then unexpectedly collapsed."

"Did your sensors record anything else?"

"No. Only the localized storm."

"Do you have the storm's perimeter?"

"Yes. It arose two kilometers from the canyon's entrance."

"Any ideas?"

"Not enough data."

"Noted. Hennesee out."

When she returned to the dig, Commander Dan glanced sharply at her. "It is not advisable to go out alone into the desert," he reproved her.

Sabrina smiled faintly. "Acknowledged. Were you aware of the storm?" she asked.

"Of course."

"Was that all you saw?" she asked. Then, more sharply, "Did you notice anything other than the storm?"

"No. Why?"

"There was another phenomena associated with the whirlwind. You didn't notice the tanks and airplanes?"

Dan looked at her as if she had lost her mind. "I heard the transmission between you and Somar. Like him, I am curious about the phenomena. His instruments only showed what I expected, the storm."

I don't like it," she muttered, shaking her head. "This phenomenon occurred without any conditions for a storm. Somar reported it came up quickly within two kilometers of the canyon, which makes it somewhat suspicious."

"Agreed."

"And the storm was all you saw?"

"As I told you."

Sabrina scratched her head. Abruptly, she ordered, "Come with me."

They walked toward the rock where she had been sitting earlier while contemplating the desert. She swung her tricorder in a semi circular motion. Nothing registered. Dan looked at her questioningly. "Let's get a ground vehicle and ride out to that rock formation," Sabrina said, and pointed to the low and worn mountain range rising from the desert floor.

Nearing the base of a cliff, Sabrina's tricorder produced a blip. It had detected a trace of energy. She exited from the vehicle and waved for Dan to follow. The reading led to a path which further up became an obstacle course of broken boulders and gullies. After numerous climbs and descents, they abruptly came upon a steep stairway leading down, which eventually took them to a shadowy cave entrance.

Cautiously, they entered. It seemed to be a labyrinth. Their flashlights showed tunnels leading off in every direction. Dan asked, "Which tunnel?" When he made ready to jump across the closest fissure, Sabrina reached out and pulled him back.

"What is it?" he asked, astonished. This was the first time ever Sabrina had touched him.

"Look," she said, and pointed. "See the rim across, it's uneven. It doesn't match up with the rest of the floor."

"Yes," he said, and looked at her with an arched eyebrow.

As an answer, Sabrina picked up a pebble and tossed it across. It went through the rim where his foot would have landed had he jumped.

"How did you know?"

"When your light struck it at an angle, I caught a shimmer."

They retraced their path to the entrance and took a different tunnel, but more carefully, now wary of possible traps. Soon the tunnel forked and they chose to go left, but it came to a dead end. Returning to the entrance once more, they took the second tunnel. Soon they came to a columned entrance opening on to an enormous plaza. Amazed, they looked at each other. It was a vast cavern dwarfing them like ants. The buildings within the cavern were five to six stories high, lining several broad avenues leading toward temples and palaces. Smaller streets branched off toward houses. Daylight was streaming in through air-shafts. Dan walked up to a curiously placed empty metal frame which stood directly underneath one of the shafts.

"Captain Hennesee!" But Sabrina was already standing behind him. "During daylight hours the sun must have shone directly down this shaft," Dan said, still manipulating the metal frame.

"There must have been a mirror here to amplify the sunlight."

"That sounds logical."

As they moved around, they found other shafts with metal frames placed directly underneath. Walking around and measuring from air-shaft to air-shaft their assumption became certainty that the frames once held mirrors to reflect light into the farthest corners of the cave.

Moving father into the houses, even in here the fine red sand of the desert swirled across the floor. Sabrina made another sweep with her recorder, but it showed no life readings. Not even insect.

When Sabrina came upon another plaza, to her utter amazement she thought she heard voices. Sometimes there were little piercing cries, or low crooning. Then she heard a childlike sing-song voice and shook her head. Lively imagination, I guess, she told herself. When she looked at Dan, he, too, was listening.

To their disbelieving eyes a dark dense fog suddenly formed in front of them. When Sabrina reached out to touch it, she felt nothing. There was nothing there. Then out of it, silently moved menacing shadows, bristling with strange and brandished weapons. They were like voiceless monsters moving out of a nightmare. Then as suddenly as they had appeared, they were gone. Sabrina and Dan were left in the eerie silence of the cavern. When Sabrina looked at Dan with her mouth still partially open, he was occupied with his recorder.

"There was an energy reading while the phenomena lasted, but now it's gone. It seemed to have come from the building straight ahead." he told Sabrina.

"A holographic projection?"

"Yes."

"But why?"

"Maybe, to deter intruders?"

"Let's investigate."

"No. We will let the scientists take care of that. This is their job."

She wanted to say spoil sport, but instead allowed her disappointment to register on her face. But Dan had long ago recognized Sabrina's deliberate displays of emotions when she was thwarted or displeased. He met her look with a raised eyebrow and she agreed to follow him. As they arrived top-side, Sabrina felt faint and had to sit down. She was sure she had expended too much energy. Lately she had been falling short of the usual unlimited stamina she demanded of herself.

Dan looked at her. She had been worrying him for some time. "Sabrina!" She looked at him, astonished by his use of her first name. "I want you to see the physician. Today."

"I'm not sick. I haven't eaten for a while and have probably expended more energy than I thought I had. I'm fine."

"I will talk to doctor Bansaro and see that he makes that an order."

* * *

Sabrina knew it was not wise to ignore Commander Dan's threat. He most likely would have doctor Bansaro order her to take a physical. When she entered sick bay, Bansaro's behavior was suspect. He definitely had been expecting her.

The doctor greeted her with typical no-nonsense Chiron firmness, telling her to undress behind the screen and then to lie down on the diagnostic table. "The nurse will come in now, and I will be back shortly."

"Yes, Doctor Bansaro," Sabrina said meekly, then, smiled at his retreating back. As though it had been choreographed, the nurse came through the door just as the doctor left and silently, but very efficiently helped Sabrina get ready.

When Bansaro came back into the room, Sabrina lifted her head as a fleeting smile crossed her face. "I surmise that Commander Dan has communicated with you.

"Yes. He has been concerned about you for some time."

The examination was short. Doctor Bansaro's eyes ran down the diagnostic read-out, and he thoughtfully rubbed his chin. Her green eyes followed his every movement. She was puzzled by his behavior and wondered what he had found. He scrutinized her for a moment then cleared his throat. "The best way to put this is straight forward; Captain Hennesee, you are pregnant."

"I am whaaa…t?" Sabrina was speechless.

"You are more than six, but not quite seven months along."

"You must be kidding!"

"Chiron's do not kid," he told her dead-pan.

Sabrina was thunderstruck. This was something that had not even occurred to her. She had been unwell for some time, but had shrugged it aside expecting it to eventually pass. She noticed the slight expansion at her waist despite losing weight, and her slacks had been getting tighter. She wrote it off as a lack of exercise, since most of the time she felt nauseous.

"You don't seem to be very comfortable with your condition?" Bansaro asked her.

Minutes ticked by, and her face grew tight. Propping herself up on her elbow, she looked at him with consternation. "If you want to know, it's a shock," she told him. "I never thought that I could be pregnant. I have no time for an infant."

He looked at her with obvious concern. "Well, it's a bit too late. You are pregnant, and this is a fact you will have to deal with. You will have a son. Also there seems to be some problem I don't understand since I'm not familiar with obstetrics, or pediatrics. I will need to take a blood sample. Also, for this stage of pregnancy, the infant appears smaller than it ought to be."

When she left sickbay, Sabrina was not happy. Again, her plans were being turned in an undesired direction. The only good news was, she was not having an incurable disease. But pregnant! It had never entered her mind. She began to feel resentful. "What a mess," she grumbled.

Three days later Bansaro called her into his office. His face looked very somber. "Captain Hennesee, you should have been under the care of an obstetrician a long time ago. Your body has developed antibodies against your child's blood. This child needs a complete blood transfusion either before it is born or immediately after."

With great difficulty, Sabrina kept her emotions under control. "That would mean terminating my command and leaving as soon as possible." After she left his office and the door closed behind her, Sabrina stood still and looked bleakly at the opposite gray wall. Her frustration was being followed swiftly by anger. Then, for the first time, real concern for the child surfaced. She went in search of Commander Dan and found him on the bridge.

"Commander, you will have to take over the Trefayne. I have to leave on a medical emergency. Also, I need to send a message to Captain Thalon."

"I have already done so. Captain Thalon is neither on the Antares nor the Explorer, and he was not reachable from Daugave. The Argos is coming in two weeks to bring supplies. She will be going into the Hyades and stopping at Madras. I have sent a message to the Explorer to have you picked up at Madras."

"Your efficiency is very commendable Commander Dan. I thank you."

Commander Dan's reply was a simple statement, "A child's life is at stake."

Sabrina walked slowly to her cabin, deep in thought. She dropped down on the edge of her bed, shoulders sagging. She shuddered and closed her eyes, then ran her hands gingerly across her abdomen. For the first time since learning of the pregnancy, it began to sink in. I am pregnant, she thought, and stared in wonderment at her belly. I am going to have a son. And then in awe, I'm going to have Sargon's son.

Chapter 18

Two weeks later, Sabrina left on the Argos. Before she left she overheard Bansaro give a briefing to the Argos' physician on her condition. The instructions were for her to rest as much as possible and to eat three meals a day.

"Doctor Bansaro, what kind of impression are you giving the doctor of the Argos," Sabrina chided him.

"The impression that you are a very busy captain and don't often think to eat unless you are reminded to do so."

Sabrina gave him an uncertain look. "I hope the doctor doesn't see me as a scatter-brained female." The Argos was from Madras. She already had a taste of the Madrians on the Corvus. They were too much taken with their superior male image, she thought. But on the Corvus she had been in command.

"I think you can handle it," Bansaro assured her.

* * *

After four days on the Argos, Sabrina had her fill of Captain Reza and being treated like an inconsequential female. She was not permitted on the bridge and was being patronized at every turn. Her requests were simply ignored and her status as an unmarried and pregnant woman had spread throughout the ship. Walking down the corridors, there were whispers and grins; she sensed the indecent hand gestures behind her back. She was also requested to forgo her uniform and was given a long, loose dress to hide her pregnancy, and her rank. Apparently, it was deemed immodest to reveal her condition.

One day she saw Reza in the officer's mess and quickly made her way to the bridge. "Lieutenant," she said, smiling sweetly and bowing humbly, "Could you please help me find the Explorer? I need to contact their Captain. It is important." She acted flustered with her hands hovering protectively above her belly.

The Lieutenant was appeased by the deference she showed. He sent the signal she gave him to contact the Explorer. When the Explorer's captain came on screen, to Sabrina's dismay, it was the face of a stranger.

"I'm Captain Hennesee and I have requested a transfer to your ship. Would it not be more convenient for the transfer to be made mid-point than by going all the way to Madras?"

"Yes, it would indeed be more convenient …" He stopped abruptly as a commotion broke out behind her. Captain Reza had come onto the bridge.

"You are forbidden to be on the bridge," he said to Sabrina as she turned around.

Sabrina turned back to the screen, "Captain?"

"Mubaric," he supplied.

"Thank you. Captain Reza. Captain Mubaric feels it would be more convenient to meet the Argos mid-point for the transfer," Sabrina relayed quickly before he could launch into a tirade.

"Is that so?" Reza asked. Honey could have dripped from his lips as he looked at the Explorer's captain. "But Madras has better medical facilities then the Antares could possibly have."

"Captain Reza, it is not the facility but the blood type that's important. My child needs a complete blood transfusion. Only Captain Thalon's blood type will match. He is the father of my child."

Captain Reza looked at her surprised. Captain Thalon, he thought, resting his fists on his hips. He had no desire to tangle with him, having met him once. Reza's was convinced, Thalon, if provoked, could be a formidable adversary. "If it is more agreeable…we will meet you mid-point," he acceded, thinking it will be a blessing to have this annoying female off my ship.

Captain Mubaric gave him the speed and position where his ship would be in eight hours, which would intersect with the Argos' path.

* * *

When Sabrina beamed over to the Explorer, she learned there had been no contact from Sargon, either to the Argos or Explorer, and the scout she had hoped to use, was missing. Several days later the Explorer's physician told her that the baby's condition was becoming critical. "If your baby does not receive the blood transfusion soon, you will lose him," he advised her.

Frantic, she sent out a coded distress signal to the Scouts. After several hours, Sargon finally answered.

She tried to stay calm, but her agitation was clearly audible in her voice, "Sargon, this is Sabrina. I'm on the Explorer, and I need you."

"State your problem."

"Oh God," she whispered. Then using the distress code, she sent, "Sargon, Sargon, priority one, priority one. I need you to come."

There was a minute pause, and then he said, "Send homing signal."

Sabrina called down to sick bay and told them to prepare for a blood transfusion for the baby, and if necessary, a caesarean section.

It took the Scout five minutes to accelerate and five to decelerate. When he beamed aboard, he was at a run. He knew when Sabrina used the priority signal there was a dire need. He found Captain Mubaric waiting for him.

"Where is she?" he asked when he didn't see Sabrina.

"She's in sickbay prepped for surgery. She's pregnant and the doctor fears that she is losing the child."

Both men were at a run when they arrived at Sickbay. In the operating room, Sabrina was already under the sheet and sedated.

Sargon looked at the doctor.

"Captain," he addressed Sargon. "I have never performed a Caesarean."

"It's all right. I will do it." Sargon studied the diagnostic readout. Using his PSI awareness, he located the infant. Then with more surety than he felt, he cut into Sabrina's abdomen. The infant was in severe distress, he could feel it. When he lifted the tiny body from its mother's womb, he knew he might be too late. He asked the other physician to take care of Sabrina. When he obtained an affirmative, he focused his attention exclusively on reviving his son. Sabrina's son, he thought as he looked at him. *So tiny, my hand nearly spans his body lengthwise.* Asking the nurse for assistance, he immediately began to transfuse his blood directly to the infant.

In the mean time, Sabrina subconsciously aware of the baby's distress had been fighting the anesthetic, trying to shake it off. She had to be put under twice. There was a frantic call from the doctor, "Captain Thalon." When Sargon looked at him, "She's fighting; she won't stay under."

"Hold her just a minute." Going down in the levels of his mind, he came in touch with Sabrina. Sargon told her, "Sabrina, listen. I'm here. Don't fight the doctor. I have the baby. He is going to be all right."

Her struggle to gain consciousness ebbed slowly, then ceased.

Lastly, Sargon disconnected himself and put his son into the incubator. He examined the boy, who seemed to be improving. There were more responses, and the skin tone was less blue.

When Sarah tested to see if he could father a child with the Original Four, she failed to tell him it was never tested against Sabrina's blood type. Had he known, he would never have let her leave the Antares.

* * *

Sabrina was a long time in recovery. Even after the anesthetic had worn off, she continued to sleep. When she finally awoke, she felt groggy, and it took a while before she became aware of her surroundings. Her first words were, "The baby?"

"He's all right. He's right here," Sargon assured her.

Sabrina's eyes followed him, as he went to the incubator to get their son. His responsiveness had improved, and his skin color was now normal with a slight golden tinge. After he was put into her arms, she pushed the blanket aside to get her first look at him. Her initial thought was, *oh my God, is he ugly,* but what she voiced was, "He's so tiny." His skin was pulled tightly across his face, and his buttocks were almost non-existent. She could count every bone in his body because he was skin and bones. *No wonder I didn't look pregnant.*

Sargon perceived her first thought, then, smiled wryly. "He nearly didn't make it," he told her.

Sabrina drew a slow, deep breath and mournfully said," I didn't know I had him."

"Yes, you did. It wasn't convenient to be pregnant, so your mind denied it when your body tried to tell you otherwise. You need to bond with the baby immediately. He's still not out of the woods yet. He is only four pounds." Perceiving her worried thoughts, he added, "I have already given him the blood-transfusion."

She let go a sigh of relief and attempted to bond. Very gently she touched his mind, but he resisted the intrusion and she had to back off. When she looked at Sargon, he told her, "Give him time."

Sargon watched as Sabrina tucked the child more comfortably into the crook of her arm. As his gaze rested on his son, he noticed a slight attempt to root.

Sabrina chuckled as she watched Sargon expose her breast to guide his mouth to the source. Feeling his feeble attempt to suckle, she willed the muscle in her breast to contract and the fluid began oozing out. Looking up, she smiled, and found an answering smile on Sargon's face.

Suddenly her eyebrows drew together as she gazed at him, searching his face. "Sargon, there was something…I saw it in your mind. You were trying to hide something from me! What have you done?" she asked, growing agitated.

"Sabrina," he said, softly, then, hesitated as the door slowly opened.

Sabrina felt a familiar presence entering the room. She looked past him until her searching eyes fell on Chantar. She was wondering why she was on the Explorer, and not on Acheron. "What are you doing here? Chan?" she asked, using the endearment she had used back on Acheron.

Chantar, after hearing Sabrina's frantic voice, had beamed over to the Explorer with Sargon to be with her friend. She had kept watch at Sabrina's bed side, and only left because Sargon thought it best if Sabrina saw him first. He had asked her to come back a little later.

Scowling again, Sabrina looked at Chantar and then at Sargon. "It has to do with Chantar," she said. "Sargon!"

His voice was terse when he said, "Sabrina, Chantar is my wife."

At first Sabrina just stared. It couldn't be, so it didn't registered. But slowly it began to dawn. "Your wife?" she whispered. Her eyes filled with tears until she could no longer see his face. She closed them and sank back into the pillow.

His amber eyes were filled with profound sorrow as he looked down at her. When he took the baby, she didn't resist. She only turned her face away.

"Sargon?" Chantar whispered.

Sargon's gaze never wavered as he held Chantar's eyes and through their bond he sent, "She will be all right."

With infinite gentleness Chantar took Sabrina's hands, and held them as she repeated, "Sabrina, please, Sabrina, please." Then, she began to weep piteously.

Chantar's crying penetrated Sabrina's numbness. She slowly turned and reluctantly opened her eyes. "Don't Chan, don't cry," she said, her voice only a dry whisper.

"Sabrina, she didn't know," Sargon broke in.

Her eyes went to Sargon with a long probing search. When she reached for him, he handed the baby to Chantar, then, allowed Sabrina's hand to rest on his forehead and their minds joined. There was a tangle of misunderstandings that she began to unravel. Sargon allowed the mind-meld to reveal a great deal about him and who he was. Much was forgiven. Now she understood the love he held for her and for the others. She realized what the children of the Antares meant to him. She looked up at him and managed a smile. "Someday, Sargon," she teased him, trying to ease the tension.

"Someday you will get even with me?" Sargon was not amused. He still remembered the day he had come very close to pushing Sabrina to the edge. It was the day he had sent her to Acheron.

"Yes. You have only so much leeway," and showed him a hair's breath between her fingers.

Cracking a smile, he promised, "Sabrina, I will stay just that far off."

Chantar gently touched the baby's head. There were tears in her eyes when she said, "Your son, Sabrina," and handed him to her.

As Sabrina looked at him, he opened his eyes, and she saw the tawny tiger eyes. Immediately, she smiled, and it lit up her whole face. She looked up at Sargon. "He has your eyes," she accused him.

"Of course. They are genetically dominant," he told her.

Very gently she tried again to link with the baby's mind, and this time he accepted the intrusion. His body might have been frail, but the mind she met was strong and full of life. She cradled him in her arms and enveloped him with her love. Suddenly there was a powerful presence beside her and she heard a voice in her mind, "I am Logan," and then the acknowledgment, "Mother."

Shock registered on Sabrina's face as she looked up at Sargon. He too had perceived the same phenomena. "It's your son's personality, or soul, if you want to call it that. He acknowledged you, and indicated that he will stay." When she gave him a confused look, he said, "He has decided not to withdraw. Mothers on my world bond with their children while pregnant. Since you didn't acknowledge the pregnancy, he wasn't sure that you wanted him."

For quite a while she was unable to say anything as she looked down into his tiny face. After she gained a vestige of composure she asked, awed, "They can withdraw if they feel they're not wanted?"

"Yes. On my world children are treated as welcomed guests, and you should only have a guest when you are prepared to receive him or her."

"Well then, Sargon, receive Logan." And she handed the child to him.

Sargon gave her an amused look, then he too mind-melded with the baby and soon was chuckling. "I think I like this little fellow," he told her and sat down on the bed. He bent down, and kissed her fully on the mouth. For the first time he lowered his barrier enough to allow his love to flow freely between them. "Thank you for a beautiful son. And please don't withhold your friendship from Chantar."

When Sargon rose, Chantar sat down on the edge of the bed, her face still wet from crying. "Sabrina, please forgive me. I didn't know that you were in love with Sargon, and he didn't know that we were friends."

"Chan, don't. After reading his mind, I understand why he and I could never be mates." Then she smiled at her. "If anyone is to have him, I'm glad it is you."

"Are you two finished bandying me about? Now, drink this," he ordered, offering her a glass.

Taking the glass, "What have you got in here, some kind a poison?" Sabrina asked, making her voice sound gruff.

"Yes. So you will go to sleep. Now give me that bundle," Sargon said, reaching for his son.

"What are you going to do with him?"

"For transfer, I want him to be in an incubator, so don't argue and drink."

Sabrina looked at him over the glass, and gingerly took a sip.

"It contains proteins, vitamins and something to make you go to sleep."

"All right, quit nagging at me." She emptied the glass and handed it to Chantar.

While Sargon put Logan into the incubator, Chantar sat beside Sabrina, stroking her hand until she drifted off to sleep.

Chapter 19

Sabrina knew she had to wake up. Rising to consciousness was like working through molasses. There was a need. Someone needed her. A small life spark was searching for her. I hate nightmares, she thought, and abruptly came awake. Instantly she smelled wood, beeswax, and the sweet scent of flowering shrubs. She knew where she was. Acheron! She didn't want to be here. "Oh, no. Oh, no," she moaned and jerked upright. She would have fallen off the bed if strong hands hadn't restrained her.

"It's all right, Sabrina. You're home," Lahoma kept assuring her.

"No, I'm not home. This is not home. I want to go home," Sabrina repeated and pushed Lahoma away. Then she became irritated. She could hear a mewing sound and was about to tell Lahoma to take care of that cat when she realized what she was hearing was her son crying. "Logan?" she said, and her head turned toward the sound. "Where is he?"

"He is in an incubator," Lahoma told her.

"Give him to me."

"I will see ..." She turned as the door opened. "Ah, here's the nurse. Lady Sabrina would like to have her baby," Lahoma told her.

"I don't think it is a good idea. The baby has been fussy all day, and it will only disturb him if he's taken out of the incubator," she said brusquely. When Lahoma turned back toward Sabrina, a pair of blazing green eyes met hers. "Sabrina, she might know better..."

Sabrina interrupted and demanded, "Throw her out."

"My, my, my, aren't we testy," another voice interjected. Karsten had come in. "What is this child doing in the incubator?" he demanded.

"Mister…"

"Doctor Karsten," he said for the benefit of the nurse and went to release Logan from his confinement. Turning to Lahoma, "The baby is bonded to his mother, and he needs to be with her at all times," he explained.

Agitated, the nurse tried to take Logan from him. "The child needs to be in the incubator," she countermanded, and pointed to it. "He has lost more weight and can't afford to lose any more. His vital signs are weaker since this morning, and he is refusing to take nourishment."

"Because you took him away from his mother," Karsten told her. "You know it is normal for babies to lose weight after they're born." He sensed her sincere concern and tried to be patient with her. She was only doing what she was trained to do, but naturally didn't understand the special needs of this child. "Lahoma, would you prop Sabrina up on her pillows?" Karsten asked.

While Lahoma fluffed Sabrina's pillows, Karsten handed Logan to her. Sabrina situated him more comfortably in her arm and began to hum a lullaby while she caressed his head. When he opened his eyes, she said, "Hello Logan, hello Sweetie," and gently began to stroke his cheek. He responded by turning his head and she opened the front of her nightgown and offered him her breast.

"Lady, he doesn't know how to," the nurse told her.

Sabrina only gave her an enigmatic smile. Once again she contracted the muscles in her breast and the milk began oozing out. Ineptly, he tried to suckle and swallow, then, his eyes opened wide. Hey, I've done this before, they seemed to say, and his efforts became more purposeful.

"Well I'll be …Sorry," the nurse apologized.

"That's all right," Karsten told her. "Those little buggers are full of surprises."

"Is this Grand Central Station?" Sabrina complained as the door opened and Tomas entered quietly. Sabrina looked at him a little closer, "Tomas," she said, and held out her hand to him. He seemed to have shrunk and looked very subdued. She had never seen him like this. He took her hand and their eyes met. Sabrina scanned him and read his grief. His daughter had died. "Tomas, I'm so sorry. My condolences."

"Thank you, Lady," he replied, very unsurprised that she knew.

"What happened?"

"She died in childbirth, Lady Sabrina."

She contemplated him for a moment, then peremptorily said, "Tomas, hand me a diaper. This boy is wet."

Tomas gave her a weak smile and did as she asked.

"Lahoma, I won't be needing a nurse. Tomas can take care of me from now on."

"Are you sure?" she asked, but looked at Karsten.

"She'll be okay," Karsten assured her. "Now, everybody out; my patient needs some rest. Tomas, why don't you go down to the kitchen and get her something to eat? Something light, like chicken soup, perhaps?"

When Tomas looked questioningly at him, Karsten smiled, "It's a universal restorative." After everyone had left, he told Sabrina, "Pull up your nightgown."

"Are you trying to get fresh?" she asked him.

"Sabrina cut the bunk and lay flat." When she complied, Karsten's hand halted above the incision Sargon had made. His face took on a vacant look while his consciousness descended to cell level, healing the cut from the inside out. "Sabrina, now out with it. What was this psychic tantrum all about before I came in?"

"What do you mean?"

"Don't equivocate with me. You nearly screamed the house down. You're lucky that I was the only one who could hear. I'm not as ethical as Sargon. If you don't tell me, I can force rapport with you."

"Karsten!" even as she looked at him, she knew he would do it, "Okay, but first take the baby away, or shield him."

"I will shield him." Karsten put his hand on Sabrina's brow. "Oh my God!" he exclaimed after he took his hand away. He read the fury and hatred Machir Aram's rape had left her with, and her consequent flight from the house of Sandor. "Why didn't you tell Sargon?"

"Tell him what, Karsten?"

"I understand. Will you tell Lahoma?"

"If anyone will tell Lahoma, it will be Machir Aram. Where did Sargon run off to?"

"He said something about going after Sarah."

"What you mean?"

"He's bringing her home."

"To the Antares?"

"Yes."

"You're short with words, Karsten. What's going on?"

"She was married, but it didn't work out. She asked Sargon to take her home." Changing the conversation he said, "If you don't want to stay here, I have the use of Chantar's chateau. Would you feel easier there?"

She gave Karsten a long probing look and sensed that there was more to this story about Sarah then he was telling her. She knew he wouldn't budge, so she simply agreed, "Yes, Karsten, please. I'm familiar with Chantar's chateau. I stayed there once before." And it had been a happy time, she thought and smiled.

* * *

Summer in the mountains meant warm, sunny days and cool nights. Sabrina enjoyed riding in the sunshine atop the light brown mare. Logan rested secure in the hammock-sling, hanging over her shoulder. He had gained weight and was growing healthier and bigger. There was much that had healed within Sabrina.

Riding single file and at a light canter, Chantar and she rode over a verdant hilltop. The air was soft. Even as early as this morning, there had been not a touch of frost. The valley stretching before them was rich with crops growing in the fields; the trees still heavy with fruit. Along the roadside, flowers bloomed. All this land belonged to Chantar's family. She was the only living female descendant in her mother's family.

A rider appeared over a fold in the meadow. "Sargon," Sabrina said and pointed.

"Yes." Chantar knew. After their marriage ceremony, alone in his room, they had bonded before he ever touched her. Now they were telepathically linked. He told her that his mind would merge with hers in a very deep meld. At first he only touched the surface of her mind. When he began to probe deeper there was the instinct to pull back, but she trusted him. Now they were joined. She had never dreamt that such closeness and happiness could exist. He was always a part of her, and she of him.

When Sargon came closer, Sabrina grumbled, "I hope he's riding a Clydesdale."

"What's a Clydesdale?"

Sabrina's mouth twitched. "It's a very large horse that wouldn't break under his weight."

Chantar laughed. The sound was so light and happy it pulled on Sabrina's heart. She quickly shut down the envious feeling and tried to be pleased for her friend.

"Hello, you two," Sargon said, as he rode up close. He pointed to Sabrina's sling. "What's that? A sack of potatoes?"

"Your son, and he is still sleeping. I'll meet you at the house." She repositioned Logan toward the front so he was supported by her arm, and pressing the flanks of her horse, galloped off.

Being with Sargon still evoked powerful emotions. There was the longing to be with him. Often she wanted to touch him, wishing it so intensely it was a physical effort not to. Only for such a short span of time had he been hers. She had given him all of her mind and all of her soul… and then, he had pulled away, and it was as it had always been. He had distanced himself and she was left with a void.

Logan squirmed. Even deep in his sleep he picked up his mother's emotions and began to cry, flailing his hands. She came back as from a far distance and heard a keening, then realized that the sound came from her. Even the mare, being made jittery, had stopped and was stomping her feet. Sabrina looked at Logan and immediately realized what had happened. She lifted him out of the sling and crooned soothingly to him until he went back to sleep.

"Poor baby," she thought," you have such a mess for a mother."

* * *

Later that evening with her emotions locked under tight control she came down to join Chantar and Sargon for dinner. She was dressed in a long gown, and her honey colored hair touched her cheeks. Entering the dining room, she only saw Sargon. She handed Logan to him with, "He has eaten and he burped. But you better use this," and put a piece of cloth over his shoulder.

Sargon bowed slightly. "Thank you, Lady Sabrina," he said. Gently patting his son's back, his face broke into a broad smile. "He has grown nicely."

"Yes, he finally looks like a baby."

"Chantar tells me that you two have written a piece of music together. She also informed me that you have a beautiful contralto. Will you sing for me tonight?"

"Sargon, it is hard for me to be around you, but I rejoice in your happiness."

Before he could answer, Chantar entered the room, glowing and radiant. She was beautiful, and Sabrina could see Sargon responding. Unaware, she had let out a sigh. When Sargon turned a questioning eye to her, she said, "I'm going back to Chambray, tomorrow."

"Sabrina, I have to leave. Why not have a pleasant evening? Come, let's eat and then you two must sing to Logan and me, all right?"

* * *

The next morning Sargon came into her room to pick up Logan. At the breakfast table he returned the baby to her. When he was ready to leave, Sabrina took Chantar by the hand. Using the old ritual of relinquishing a male to an opponent she said, "Chantar, this male, he is yours."

Chantar's eyes danced with mirth as she broke into a wide grin. "Sabrina, I accept. This male, he is mine."